MAU LIN TOWER

Westminster Public Library
3705 W 112th Ave
Westminster, CO 80031
www.westminsterlibrary.org

Also by Chris Priestley...

Maudlin Towers: Curse of the Werewolf Boy

*

Uncle Montague's Tales of Terror
Tales of Terror from the Black Ship
Tales of Terror from the Tunnel's Mouth

*

Mister Creecher
Through Dead Eyes
The Dead Men Stood Together
The Last of the Spirits

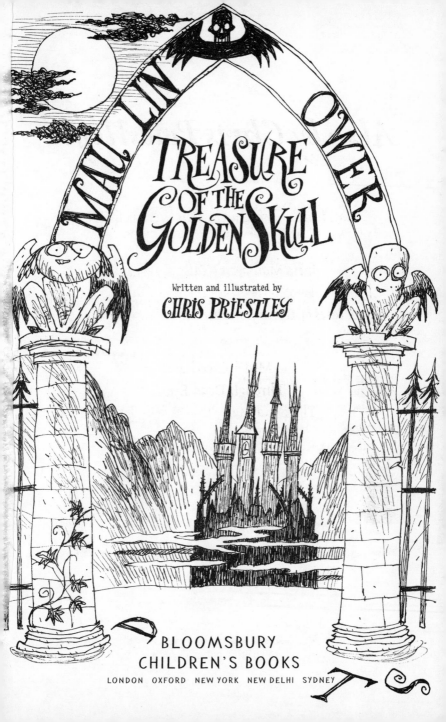

MAUDLIN TOWER

TREASURE OF THE GOLDEN SKULL

Written and illustrated by

CHRIS PRIESTLEY

BLOOMSBURY
CHILDREN'S BOOKS

LONDON   OXFORD   NEW YORK   NEW DELHI   SYDNEY

BLOOMSBURY CHILDREN'S BOOKS
Bloomsbury Publishing Plc
50 Bedford Square, London, WC1B 3DP, UK

BLOOMSBURY, BLOOMSBURY CHILDREN'S BOOKS and the
Diana logo are trademarks of Bloomsbury Publishing Plc

First published in Great Britain in October 2018 by Bloomsbury Publishing Plc
Text and illustrations copyright © Chris Priestley, 2018

A catalogue record for this book is available from the British Library

ISBN: PB: 978-1-4088-7310-6; eBook: 978-1-4088-7311-3

2 4 6 8 10 9 7 5 3 1

Typeset by RefineCatch Limited, Bungay, Suffolk

Printed and bound in Great Britain by CPI Group (UK) Ltd, Croydon CR0 4YY

MIX
Paper from
responsible sources
FSC® C020471

To find out more about our authors and books visit www.bloomsbury.com
and sign up for our newsletters

Mildew and Sponge were just walking past the Headmaster's office on the way back from their twice-weekly jog up the side of Pig's Pike with their appallingly energetic new sports teacher, Mr Lithely, when they heard a terrible crash and saw a cloud of dust emerge from under the door.

They rushed inside and gasped in horror. One of the pinnacles from somewhere in the cloud-swaddled heights of Maudlin Towers had broken off and plummeted through the ceiling of the Headmaster's office, embedding itself in his desk. Part of the Headmaster's gown was visible sticking out from under it.

'Headmaster!' shouted the boys.

Miss Pernickety, the school secretary, ran in,

saw the wreckage and the Headmaster's gown, screamed and swooned into Mildew and Sponge's outstretched arms.

'I am quite all right,' said a familiar voice behind them.

They turned to see the Headmaster, his gown ripped asunder, standing on the other side of the room, smiling as usual, but shaking his head as he stared at the damage to his office.

Miss Pernickety recovered her senses immediately, got to her feet, straightened her clothes and disappeared back to her office without a word.

To Mildew and Sponge's astonishment, the Headmaster heaved a sigh, wandered across to his chair by the fire, sat down and proceeded to blub pitifully. The boys stared, mouths agape. It was too shocking.

They tried to leave without becoming involved any further, but too late. The Headmaster looked up and waved them forward with a frail movement of his hand.

'Boys,' he said weakly. 'Close the door, Mildew, there's a good fellow.'

Mildew did as he was asked.

'But with you on this side of it!' called the Headmaster.

Mildew opened the door and came back into the office, closing the door behind him. He sat next to his friend by the Headmaster's hearth.

'I am most terribly sorry you had to witness this display of emotion,' said the Headmaster. 'But if you knew the cause, you would understand, I'm sure.'

'That's quite all right,' said Mildew. 'Sponge blubs all the time, don't you, Sponge?'

'I don't think I blub any more than you,' Sponge replied with a frown.

'Oh, come now,' said Mildew. 'You blub at the drop of a hat.'

'I certainly don't,' said Sponge. 'What about you, in any case? You blubbed when the moths ate your bed socks.'

'They were cashmere!' protested Mildew.

'Boys,' said the Headmaster gently but firmly. 'If I might interrupt your charming banter.'

'Yes, sir,' said Mildew. 'Sorry, sir. I expect you'd like to be alone with your thoughts. My father always likes to be alone with his thoughts when he's blubbing.'

'I've failed you, boys,' blurted the Headmaster.

'Failed us, sir?' said Sponge nervously, looking this way and that. 'How, sir? In particular, I mean?'

'I fear the school governors are planning to … shut us down,' said the Headmaster.

The boys gasped.

'Why, sir?' said Mildew.

'Well, as you can see, the building is literally falling to pieces. The school funds simply won't cover building work of the required magnitude. We need extra funds and quickly and the governors refuse to help.

'I'm afraid the new Chair of Governors is a very enthusiastic retired general – Sir Brashly Bugle. He has made it clear that we are running an old-fashioned, out-of-date institution, producing boys both soft in brain and body.

'He thinks all boys should be in a military academy, marching up and down at six o'clock every morning. He'd have us do it here if the place weren't so expensive to maintain. Instead he wants to strip the school of anything of value and build a new one elsewhere, more in line with his views.'

'Could you not sell the School Diamond?' said Sponge, shaking his head and blinking.

'That's just it. I sold it last year,' said the Headmaster. 'The so-called School Diamond in the trophy room is no more than a piece of glass from the dining-room chandelier. I had the money. I was about to engage the builders this month. They had put me off and put me off and we had finally arranged a date and then ...'

'Sir?' said Mildew.

'I'm afraid I have never trusted banks, you see. I could have simply looked after the money here – I have a safe in this office – but I have a terrible compulsion to buy shoes. I can't stop myself. We are all weak in our own ways, boys.'

'Shoes?' said Sponge.

'Where?' said the Headmaster expectantly.

'What about the money, sir?' said Mildew, frowning.

The Headmaster put his head in his hands.

'I placed it in the care of a person whose honesty was beyond reproach and who I knew would never allow me to change my mind about buying shoes.'

'Who, sir?' asked Mildew and Sponge in unison.

'Reverend Brimstone.'

The boys nodded. That made sense.

'But I'm afraid that Reverend Brimstone chose an unfortunate place to hide the money,' said the Headmaster forlornly. 'A place he had every reason to believe might be safe. A place where the money would always be under his very ...'

'Oh no,' said Sponge.

'His chair!' said Mildew.

'Indeed,' said the Headmaster. 'And, as we all know, it was stolen. The good reverend still mourns for that chair, you know.'

At that moment Reverend Brimstone himself walked past the Headmaster's office, muttering wildly. The only words audible were 'chair', 'thief' and 'burning in the pits of hell for all eternity'.

Mildew and Sponge both had an image in their heads of the last time they saw the chair-turned-time-machine – just before it took Mr Stupendo, their old sports teacher, back to the age of dinosaurs.

'We will perhaps never know what happened to the chair,' said the Headmaster, 'or to the fortune it contained. It's a mystery. But I wish I had the villains responsible here with me now, I don't mind telling you!'

Sponge gulped. Mildew accompanied him. The Headmaster sighed and after a moment managed to muster a faint shadow of his usual smile. Sponge gazed around the room nervously.

'Why are there barnacles attached to the wooden panelling of your office?' said Sponge. 'We are an awfully long way from the sea.'

The Headmaster walked to the wreckage and picked up a piece of wood. Sure enough, the back of it was encrusted with barnacles. The Headmaster stared off into the distance for a moment.

'Well, well,' he said. 'Look at that. After all these years.'

'Sir?' said Mildew and Sponge.

The Headmaster smiled and sat down in his chair once more, looking up at the hole in his ceiling.

'Well, boys,' he said. 'The fact of the matter is, the wood panels in my office were made from the timbers of a ship.'

Having been told, it seemed obvious. That explained the huge anchor in the corner of the room. They had always wondered why that was there.

'And not just any ship, I should add,' continued the Headmaster. 'A pirate ship! The *Golden Skull*.'

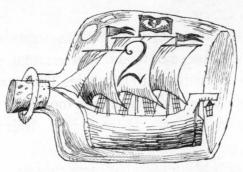

Ship in a Bottle

'The *Golden Skull*?' cried Sponge.

'Yes,' said the Headmaster. 'In fact this is the very vessel in question.'

The Headmaster stood up and took the ship in a bottle from his mantelpiece, sat back down and blew the dust from it. Sponge and Mildew coughed and spluttered.

Peering through the grimy glass, they saw a painstakingly detailed model of a three-masted sailing ship. A black flag with a winged skull in gold flew from the mainmast – the winged skull of the Maudlin Towers school badge.

'Ooh!' said Sponge.

'It was sailed by one of the most fearsome pirates of the age – Greenbeard.'

'Greenbeard?' said Mildew.

'Yes,' said the Headmaster. 'His personal hygiene was not all it might have been. That and the leaky nature of his ship meant that his beard was alive with seaweed apparently. As well as the odd hermit crab.'

'Was there any treasure at all?' said Mildew. 'Pirates are great ones for treasure, aren't they?'

'Oh yes,' said the Headmaster. 'Greenbeard was very fond of jewels in particular and collected a hoard of them, apparently. Legend has it that the treasure is buried on a far-flung island haunted by the ghost of Greenbeard himself. But no one has ever been able to locate it. It appears in no known atlas or map.'

'How frustrating,' said Sponge.

'Indeed,' said the Headmaster. 'I'm afraid the whereabouts of Greenbeard's treasure will forever remain a mystery. We could do with it now, eh, boys?'

'But why were his ship's timbers made into an office at Maudlin Towers?' said Sponge.

'Well, now,' said the Headmaster. 'That's the fascinating thing. Greenbeard the Pirate was actually from this very place. He was a local lad – a servant in this building when it was the family seat of the Maudlins. He ran away to sea with his master, Lord Mandrake Maudlin.'

'Really?' said Sponge.

The Headmaster nodded.

'As you know, Lord Mandrake's son, Lord Marzipan Maudlin, was a great collector and eccentric ...'

Mildew and Sponge knew this very well, having met Lord Marzipan Maudlin in person on their earlier time-travelling adventures.

'And, knowing the connection with his father, he managed to track down the remains of the *Golden Skull* and had it made into his office. When he decided to turn Maudlin Towers into a school, he adopted Greenbeard's flag as the school badge.

'Of course, over time, the governors took a dim view of the school's association with piracy and each successive Headmaster – myself included – was asked never to divulge it to the students. But I know I can count on you both to keep this matter strictly between ourselves. If news of the impending closure of the school spread through the cloisters and dorms, there would be complete panic. I know how much you all love this place. How much we all love it.'

Sponge and Mildew exchanged the swiftest of sceptical glances.

'Can I have a closer look at the *Golden Skull*?' asked Sponge.

The Headmaster smiled and handed him the ship in a bottle, but Sponge's grip faltered and it slipped out of his fingers like a bar of soap, falling to the floor and smashing the glass into pieces on the tiles.

'Sponge!' cried Mildew.

'Oh dear,' said the Headmaster. 'What a shame.'

Sponge picked up the model ship, now free of its glass container and lifted it up.

'I'm so sorry, sir,' said Sponge tearfully.

'Not to worry,' said the Headmaster with his usual cheery outlook. 'Accidents will happen. At least we can now have a closer look at the ship itself.'

The middle mast had come loose and Sponge tried to put it back in place. As he did so, he noticed some writing on the mainsail.

'Sir!' cried Sponge. 'I think this may be a clue to the treasure.'

'What?' said the Headmaster. 'Where?'

But as Sponge handed the ship over, the sails began to disintegrate, falling to tiny pieces.

'No!' shouted the Headmaster as the sails dissolved to dust. 'The atmosphere inside the bottle must have preserved them, but now they are decomposing.'

He banged his fist on the desk in frustration and another piece of wood panelling was shaken loose from the ceiling and fell, striking Sponge on the head and knocking him senseless for a moment or two.

'Sponge?' said Mildew, rushing to the aid of his fallen comrade. 'Are you all right?'

Sponge blinked a few times and shook his head to clear it, stars flashing in front of his eyes. He staggered to his feet and sat down in the chair once more.

'What did it say, Sponge?' said Mildew.

'What did what say?' said Sponge.

'The sail,' said Mildew. 'What did it say on the sail?'

'Yes,' said the Headmaster. 'What did it say, Spongely-Partwork? The clue on the sail? You were the only one to glimpse it.'

Sponge looked from face to face and down at the damaged ship.

'I can't remember,' said Sponge. 'Not a thing. The thwack on my head seems to have knocked it out of my brain.'

'Curses,' said Mildew.

'Perhaps it will come back in a while,' said the Headmaster, 'if you try hard to think about it.'

But when Sponge tried to recall what was written on the sail, all he could remember was the hollow *donk* of wood panelling on cranium and nothing more.

The Headmaster sighed and told them to go about the rest of their day. Mildew and Sponge solemnly left the office and walked with equal solemnity down the corridor and round the corner before bouncing around wide-eyed.

'No more Maudlin Towers, Sponge,' said Mildew dreamily. 'Can you imagine?'

'I'm trying, Mildew,' said Sponge, rubbing his head. 'Although it's awfully difficult when your brains have been battered.'

Mr Lithely bounded past, taking the time to slap each of the boys enthusiastically on the back, which sent Sponge sprawling to the floor.

'Looking forward to the next sprint up Pig's Pike, boys?' he cried as he disappeared round the corner.

'I can't say I'll miss this place,' said Mildew.

Sponge nodded as he got to his feet.

'But I suppose our parents will want us to go to another school,' said Sponge.

'What?' said Mildew, the smile fading from his face.

'Well, they won't let us just have a long holiday, will they?'

'Won't they? Oh – I suppose you're right.'

'Still,' said Sponge. 'I'm sure the new school

we go to won't be as bad as Maudlin Towers. How could it be?'

Mildew got to his feet and stared off into the distance for a longish amount of time.

'Mildew?' said Sponge. 'What is it?'

Mildew turned to face him, tears brimming in his eyes.

'But don't you see?' he said. 'We shan't go to the same school, Sponge. We shall be sent to who-knows-where and with who-knows-who.'

'Whom,' Sponge corrected him.

'Never mind that,' said Mildew. 'We have to do something.'

'But how? And also what?'

Mildew grabbed his friend by both shoulders and stared purposefully into Sponge's eyes.

'We must save the school!'

'Are you sure?'

'I am!'

3 Every Boy's Book of Pirates

Mildew and Sponge set their minds to thinking about how they might replace the money they had inadvertently sent back in time and thereby save the school.

'May I have a biscuit, Mildew?' asked Sponge wearily. 'To give my little brain a little boost.'

'Biscuit?' said Mildew. 'I'm afraid I don't have any biscuits.'

Sponge peered at him.

'What about the ones in your drawer?'

'You're rambling, Sponge,' said Mildew, examining his fingernails. 'I am utterly biscuitless, I assure you.'

'But I've seen them,' said Sponge, narrowing his eyes. 'Your mother sent them last week. They are in your drawer. If you just –'

'You're seeing things, Sponge. Now, if we can forget about your biscuit obsession for a moment and get back to the matter in hand ...'

Sponge scowled and made a whistling noise through his nose – a noise he knew Mildew found particularly annoying. Mildew pretended not to notice. After ten minutes they counted their ideas.

'So, correct me if I'm wrong, Sponge – and maths has never been my strong point, as you know – but I make that no ideas at all.'

Sponge did some mental mathematics of his own, his face contorted by concentration.

'Agreed,' he gasped. 'I, too, make it none.'

Mildew pulled at his hair and groaned.

'What are we going to do?'

'I don't know,' said Sponge with a pitiful whine. 'Perhaps we should just give up.'

Mildew stared at his friend in astonishment.

'Sponge!' cried Mildew. 'What kind of attitude is that? Did the Austrian army give up when Napoleon had them cornered in 1805?'

'Well – yes,' said Sponge. 'I think they did, if memory serves.'

'Well, did the Crusaders give up when Saladin had Jerusalem surrounded in 1187?'

'Yes,' said Sponge. 'I distinctly remember Mr Luckless telling us all about –'

'Yes, well, never mind that,' said Mildew. 'The point is, a Mildew never admits defeat!'

Sponge tried, not wholly successfully, to stop himself emitting a derisive snort. Mildew tried, with similarly mixed results, to ignore the semi-stifled wheeze.

The boys decided that, with no fundraising ideas forthcoming, they may as well head to the library and find out a little more about Greenbeard the Pirate.

Miss Foxing, the school librarian, stood at her desk, reading, her red hair shimmering in the golden light from the window above her head. She looked up as they approached.

'Miss Foxing,' said Sponge as he and Mildew ambled up to the desk. 'What would you say is the best book about pirates in the library?'

Miss Foxing thought for a moment and then opened a draw full of index cards.

'Well,' she said, 'we have: An A–Z of Pirates; A Pirate Encyclopaedia; Pirates of the World; Pirates, Pirates, Pirates; The Pirate Cook Book; I Was a Teenage Pirate; Let's All Look at Pirates ...'

She stopped at a particular card and pulled it out with a smile.

'But I would say the best – the most comprehensive – book on pirates is this one: Every Boy's Book of Pirates. You'll find it over there in the "Pirate" section.'

Mildew and Sponge couldn't think why they'd never noticed this section before. They found the book and dragged the enormous tome with some difficulty to a quiet corner and placed it across both their laps. Mildew opened it and turned to the index.

'Gingerbeard, Goatbeard, Goodbeard, Greatbeard ... Here we are: Greenbeard.'

They turned to the relevant page and there was an illustration of Greenbeard aboard the Golden Skull, his crew about him. He cut quite a figure.

Greenbeard stood on the deck, a tricorn hat on his head, a huge green beard on his face, a sash around his waist stuffed with pistols and a cutlass in both hands.

'Goodness,' said Sponge. 'There's a distinct resemblance.'

'To whom?'

'To you,' said Sponge.

'Nonsense,' said Mildew.

'It's true! If you had a large green beard and were dressed as a pirate,' said Sponge, 'I think you'd be very similar indeed.'

'Here we go again. This is just like that business with the bust you thought was you.'

'And I was right about that!' protested Sponge. 'It was me!'

Mildew stared at the illustration anew and saw that Sponge might indeed have a point. Greenbeard really did look like him.

'Maybe ...' said Mildew.

'It must just be an odd coincidence,' said Sponge.

'Of course,' said Mildew.

They read the biography and marvelled at Greenbeard's daring as he sailed the ocean, fearlessly capturing ship after ship, gathering a massive collection of treasure, which he shared among his crew – all except the jewels, which he kept for himself.

They read the biography, searching for anything about the treasure, but it just repeated what the Headmaster had said about it being buried on a far-flung, mysterious island – although it did name it as Mute Row Island.

They went to find an atlas but there was no such place listed. If there ever had been a Mute Row Island, it had long since been forgotten or renamed.

Then, as he opened *Every Boy's Book of Pirates*

again, Sponge noticed something else.

'Look,' he said.

He showed Mildew who had written the book. It was none other than Mr Luckless, their history teacher.

'Come on, Sponge!' cried Mildew.

Mr Luckless is Consulted

T he boys found Mr Luckless staring off into the middle distance, as he had been wont to do ever since he had returned Miss Livia to Roman times. They had to knock on the classroom door several times before he woke from his trance.

'Ah, boys,' he said as he waved them in. 'How nice to see you. Have you come to deliver your essays ahead of schedule?'

The boys glanced at each other.

'Er ... no, sir,' said Sponge. 'We have come to pick your brains.'

'Pick away, boys,' he said. 'Pick away.'

'We've come to talk to you about Greenbeard the Pirate.'

Mr Luckless smiled.

'So your father has decided to tell you after all, Mildew,' said Mr Luckless. 'I'm glad.'

'My father, sir?' said Mildew. 'Why would my father know anything about this piratical Greenbeard fellow? He seldom leaves the house – apart from when he goes to the bottom of the garden to sigh.'

'But I don't understand,' said Mr Luckless. 'If he hasn't told you about the family connection, why are you here?'

'What family connection, sir?' asked Mildew.

'Greenbeard was a Mildew, Mildew,' said Mr Luckless.

Mildew and Sponge gasped in surprise and turned to look at each other.

'The picture in *Every Boy's Book of Pirates!*' cried Sponge.

Mildew nodded, wide-eyed.

'I'm sorry,' said Mr Luckless. 'Oh dear. Perhaps I should not have mentioned it. It must be a terrible shock, Mildew. To have a notorious buccaneer in the family.'

'No. Not at all.' said Mildew with a smile. 'On the contrary. It's remarkable. Who would ever have imagined it? An interesting Mildew!'

'*Another* interesting Mildew,' said Sponge loyally.

Mildew smiled and placed a hand on his friend's shoulder.

'Thank you, Sponge,' said Mildew. 'But the Mildews have always hailed from Berkshire. How did this unfortunate find himself up here?'

'Apparently,' said Mr Luckless, 'the Mildews had fallen on hard times and a branch of the family was forced north to look for employment.'

'But I don't understand,' said Sponge. 'How did this Mildew ancestor come to be an unhygienic pirate and what has that to do with Maudlin Towers?'

Mr Luckless hooked his thumbs under his gown and peered over his glasses.

'Thereby hangs a tale …' he replied with an arch of his eyebrow.

'Sir?' said Mildew, after several minutes had elapsed.

'Ah. I see. You'd like to hear it?'

'If you wouldn't mind, sir,' said Sponge.

'Very well,' began Mr Luckless. 'It was two hundred years ago, now. Lord Mandrake Maudlin lived in Maudlin Towers. After a variety of disappointments, Lord Mandrake decided his fortune lay at sea and, leaving the servants in charge of Maudlin Towers and the estate, he put all his money into buying a ship.

'When I say he left the servants in charge, he didn't leave them all behind. He took a young servant lad with him. That young fellow was your ancestor, Aubrey Mildew – he who would one day become infamous throughout the seven seas as Greenbeard the Pirate.'

'I can't believe I've never been told about this,' said Mildew excitedly.

'Well, the fact is, I only discovered this very recently in the archives of Maudlin Towers whilst researching the second edition of *Every Boy's Book of Pirates*. I contacted your father in my excitement and he was most insistent that I say nothing to you – or anyone else. I assumed when you came

here that he had been in touch with you to say he had had a change of heart.'

Mildew frowned.

'Why would my father refuse to tell me?' said Mildew.

'I think he felt ashamed, Mildew,' said Mr Luckless. 'He was embarrassed. I told him there was no need, but he would not be persuaded. Personally, I think it's fascinating and I'm glad you know.

'On the other hand, please don't let on that you know – he may have me fired.'

Mildew nodded.

'Your secret is safe with me,' said Mildew.

Mr Luckless smiled.

'I know,' he said. 'We already share a few, don't we?'

'Indeed we do,' agreed Mildew. 'Although we may not be sharing many more.'

Mr Luckless frowned.

'Why do you say that?'

'Well, sir,' said Sponge, 'the fact is, the Headmaster told us he thinks the school is doomed.'

'Doomed?' said Mr Luckless, looking round. 'Not in a painful sense, I hope.'

'The governors seem intent on closing the school down, sir,' said Mildew, 'because of the generally crumbly state of the building and the scary Chair of Governors. Has the Headmaster not told you?'

'Sadly, our esteemed Headmaster does not always feel the need to tell the staff everything,' said Mr Luckless. 'Or indeed anything.'

'I think it's because he feels responsible, sir,' said Sponge.

'How so?' said Mr Luckless.

'He had the money for the renovations and lost it, sir,' said Mildew.

'Lost it?' said Mr Luckless, frowning. 'That seems very irresponsible. Where was it?'

'He gave it to Reverend Brimstone,' said Sponge, 'who hid it in his chair.'

Mr Luckless raised an eyebrow and became a shade paler.

'In his chair?' said Mr Luckless. 'The same chair that …?'

'Yes,' said Sponge.

'The one that …?'

'Indeed,' said Mildew.

'So the money is now …?'

'Quite,' said Mildew.

'So in a way it's …?'

'Mr Particle's fault,' said Mildew firmly. 'Yes, I suppose it is. Although it seems unfair to blame him when he's no longer here to defend himself, sir.'

No one spoke for a little while.

'I'll miss this place if I have to go and teach

elsewhere,' said Mr Luckless. 'I know that sounds strange. It is an appalling place in so many ways.'

'No, sir,' said Sponge. 'Mildew and I were saying the same.'

'Still. I'm sure we will all manage,' said Mr Luckless. 'Perhaps it will be no bad thing to leave some memories behind and move on to a new adventure.'

The two boys and their teacher all sat quietly for a moment, thinking about what had been and what might lie ahead. After a collective sigh, it was Mildew who broke the silence.

'I only wish I had Greenbeard's treasure. Then everything could stay the same. I could save the school and still have some spare cash to buy biscuits and so forth.'

'Some *more* biscuits,' Sponge corrected him with a frown.

Mildew ignored him.

'Sponge actually saw a clue to the whereabouts of the treasure,' said Mildew. 'On the ship in a bottle the Headmaster has in his office. But he got bonked on the old brain box and has clean forgotten it.'

'But the treasure was buried on some long-forgotten spot, wasn't it?' said Mr Luckless. 'Mute Row Island? So it's no use to anyone. Who knows where that is or was. It might cost more to travel there than the treasure is worth.'

There was another collective sigh and all three hung their heads.

'It's a curious coincidence though, isn't it, sir?' said Sponge after a few moments.

'What is, Master Spongely-Partwork?' said Mr Luckless.

'That Mute Row Island should be an anagram of Maudlin Towers,' he said.

Mildew and Mr Luckless stared at him. Such a display of mental agility was akin to seeing a cat play the harpsichord. Sponge registered their surprise.

'Oh – it's a bit of a knack I have,' said Sponge by way of explanation. 'I often help Aunt Bernard with her crossword puzzles in the hols.'

Mildew shook his head in wonder.

'But do you see what this means?' said Mr Luckless. 'Perhaps Greenbeard didn't bury his treasure on some distant island at all. Perhaps he brought it back to Maudlin Towers and buried it here.'

'But where, sir?' said Mildew. 'We're not much better off, are we, without knowing the clue that Sponge saw?'

Mr Luckless slumped back in his seat.

'You're right, of course,' he said. 'We might look for years and never find it. In some ways it is worse to think it is hiding somewhere nearby, taunting us.'

The boys nodded their agreement.

'You know that the ghostly Greenbeard is supposed to guard the treasure?' Mr Luckless said.

'G … G … Ghost?' burbled Sponge.

'Stuff and nonsense, of course,' said Mr Luckless. 'Pirates were a superstitious lot and the legend was no doubt designed to put anyone off trying to find it.'

'Schoolboys are quite superstitious too, sir,' said Sponge.

'*Some* are,' said Mildew, raising an eyebrow at his friend.

The boys left their history teacher alone and decided to head off to lunch. They had barely taken two steps away from Mr Luckless's room when Mildew spotted something.

'Look,' whispered Mildew. 'Behind that column. It's Kenningworth.'

At the sound of their voices, Kenningworth's hair retreated out of sight and by the time they reached the spot where they had seen him, Kenningworth himself had disappeared.

'What's he doing skulking about?' said Sponge. 'Do you think he heard any of what we've been talking about?'

'Who knows?' said Mildew.

The boys decided to make their way to the dining hall for lunch, where they joined the queue behind Hipflask, Filbert and Enderpenny.

'Not offal again, Mrs Glump,' said Mildew as a large gelatinous lump flopped on to his plate.

'There's nothing wrong with offal,' said Mrs Glump, wiping her nose on the back of her arm. 'This country was built on offal.'

Mildew and Sponge carried their trays to a table and sat down opposite each other. Hipflask and Enderpenny had gone to sit with Kenningworth at the next table.

'Just look at Kenningworth,' said Sponge. 'Why is he looking so smug?'

Mildew scowled. Kenningworth was indeed looking particularly pleased with himself.

'I dare say we'll find out soon enough,' said Mildew. 'But right now we have more important things on our plates.'

Sponge looked at the offal on his plate.

'Not our actual plates, Sponge,' said Mildew. 'Our metaphorical plates.'

Sponge stared at him with his mouth partly open.

'Oh, never mind,' said Mildew.

School For Pirates

Mildew awoke the following day to the sound of the birdlife of England chirruping outside his window and inside his ears. When he opened his eyes he saw the Headmaster looming over him with his crocodilian smile.

'Aghh!' said Mildew, waking Sponge.

'Aghh!' said Sponge.

'Might I ask you both to accompany me to my office?' asked the Headmaster. 'If you would be so kind. At your earliest convenience.'

The boys got out of bed, put on their slippers and followed the Headmaster to his office, where he thrust a newspaper towards them. It was the *Daily Wail*. The headline said:

SCHOOL FOR PIRATES

Ahoy there! Maudlin Towers School in Cumberland is now a school for pirates. Arthur Mildew Esq. (of the Berkshire Mildews) has discovered he is descended from the infamous pirate Green-beard, and the whole school has succumbed to pirate fever as they search for his long-lost buried treasure. What is our education system coming to? Sir Brashly Bugle, Chair of Governors at Maudlin Towers School for Pirates, was unavailable for comment.

The story continued its very unflattering – mostly fantastical – portrait of the state of affairs at Maudlin Towers. The Headmaster tapped the newspaper.

'What is the meaning of this? I thought we agreed that our little conversation would be a secret,' said the Headmaster.

'Yes,' said Sponge. 'Have you told someone, sir?'

'Have I told …? No, I have not told someone, Spongely-Partwork – *you* have told someone.'

'I most certainly have not, sir,' said Sponge.

They both turned to Mildew.

'Well, neither have I!' Mildew cried, his voice a couple of octaves higher than he had intended.

'And what's this nonsense about you being a descendant of Greenbeard?'

'I'm afraid it's true, sir,' said Mildew. 'Mr Luckless told us and … Wait a minute …'

Mildew narrowed his eyes.

'Kenningworth!'

'Of course!' cried Sponge. 'He was lurking about outside Mr Luckless's door when we left, Headmaster. He must have overheard.'

'I see,' he said, narrowing his eyes. 'Kenningworth does come from a long line of lurkers. His father was a famous lurker. I also believe one of his many uncles works for the *Daily Wail*.'

'That's why he was looking so full of himself over lunch yesterday,' said Mildew. 'He must have sold the story to the *Daily Wail*.'

'I'm afraid knowing it was Kenningworth – if indeed it was he – does not get us anywhere. In fact it only makes matters worse. His mother is on the Board of Governors, just to add to everything. I'm afraid making the connection with pirates public will not play well with the governors or parents. Now they think I'm so desperate I'm searching for treasure. It will only hasten Sir Brashly Bugle's plans to close us down.'

Mildew and Sponge left the Headmaster and headed off to breakfast, finding Kenningworth sitting with some of the other boys.

'Yo-ho-ho,' said Kenningworth, chortling like an easily amused warthog. 'Here comes Cap'n Mildew.'

'Sneak,' said Sponge. 'You were listening!'

'So? At least my ancestors weren't pirates,' said Kenningworth.

'No. Perhaps not,' said Mildew. 'I'm going to guess at some sort of rodent.'

Kenningworth bristled.

'I wish I was descended from pirates,' said Enderpenny. 'I come from a long line of sock salesmen.'

'Yes,' said Hipflask. 'What's so bad about Mildew having a pirate in his family tree? It sounds rather exciting to me.'

'There,' said Mildew. 'No one cares, Kenningworth.'

'Try to wriggle out of it all you like, Mildew,' said Kenningworth, 'but pirates are thieves when it comes down to it and no one likes a thief.'

The boys all turned to Mildew.

'That's true, isn't it, Spoon – sorry, I mean Sponge,' said Mildew.

'Why did you call me Spoon?' said Sponge. 'Oh – I see. *Spoon*. Very good.'

Kenningworth's eyes bounced back and forth like tennis balls in a doubles match. He signalled for Mildew and Sponge to come with him and they found a secluded corner near the toilets.

'You said you'd never mention that business about me and the School Spoon!' he hissed.

'That was while we'd forgotten what a stinker you are!' said Sponge.

'All right, all right,' said Kenningworth, lowering his voice. 'So what if I made some money from the pirate story? Where's the harm?'

'The school is in danger,' said Sponge. 'The Headmaster fears we might be closed down.'

'Pah!' said Kenningworth. 'Good riddance.'

'We'll all be taken to who-knows-where,' said Mildew. 'Is that what you want?'

'Yes. I hate it here,' said Kenningworth. 'And now, to make matters worse, my dear mother has become a governor at the school. Do you know what that means? It means she gets to nose around at Maudlin Towers whenever she sees fit. She'll speak to the Headmaster. Can you imagine?'

The boys had to admit that they saw Kenningworth's point on this. The horror of a marauding parent was all too real.

'But even so,' said Sponge, 'you can't want to see all your friends dispersed.'

'Friends?' said Kenningworth bitterly, turning away. 'I don't have any real friends and you know it.'

'I'm sure that's not true,' said Mildew very unconvincingly.

Kenningworth looked at his feet.

'Has your mother said anything about visiting the school?' said Sponge. 'In a school governory kind of way?'

Kenningworth nodded.

'Imminently,' he said, turning round.

The boys gasped. Kenningworth chuckled to himself.

'You don't seem unduly concerned,' remarked Mildew.

'Well, the fact is my mother has, for a long time, considered Maudlin Towers an inappropriate match for my various talents and sensibilities.'

'Haven't we all,' said Mildew.

'She has been looking at schools on the Continent,' said Kenningworth, ignoring Mildew. 'There's one in the south of France that looks particularly comfortable – Le Petit Prince. The sooner this place closes down the better. No more hail and snow for me, boys. I shall be dipping my toes in the warm, azure water of the Mediterranean!'

Kenningworth wandered off, whistling.

Felicity Fallowfield Strikes Again

At break time, Mildew and Sponge went back to the library but *Every Boy's Book of Pirates* provided no more clues as to where Greenbeard's treasure might be. Sponge tried once again to coax his brain into remembering what had been written on the sails of the *Golden Skull* and, as often happened when Sponge coaxed his brain to do anything, he fell fast asleep. When he awoke he found Mildew reading a newspaper.

'Why are you reading the *Daily Wail*, Mildew?' said Sponge in disgust. 'Don't encourage them.'

'Shhhh!' said Miss Foxing.

'Felicity Fallowfield has struck again,' whispered Mildew. 'She stole the Infanta of Fandango's emerald. Right from under her nose. Which is huge, apparently.'

47

'The emerald or the nose?' said Sponge.

'It doesn't make that clear.'

'Who is Felicity Fallowfield?' said Sponge.

'Really, Sponge,' said Mildew. 'You must endeavour to be better informed about the wither and thither of life. Felicity Fallowfield: arch-criminal and master of disguise. She is the most glamorous twelve-year-old in the Empire – possibly in the entire known world.'

'I'm surprised you see the doings of an arch-criminal as heroic, Mildew,' said Sponge with a mischievous grin. 'Perhaps Kenningworth was right about your piratical leanings.'

Mildew put his newspaper down and, seeing Miss Foxing scowling at them, suggested they continue the conversation elsewhere.

'I don't say she is a hero, Sponge,' said Mildew as they walked. 'One can't condone her thievery, of course, but one simply has to admire her nerve, her verve. She'd have found the treasure of the *Golden Skull* in a jiffy and still have time to ruffle our hair, tweak our noses and stamp on our toes as she was making her escape.'

'I don't want my toes tweaked,' said Sponge.

'Noses,' said Mildew. 'Not toeses. I mean toes. Oh, never mind.'

'What are we going to do?' said Sponge.

'I don't know, Sponge,' said Mildew. 'How's your head?'

'Better, thank you.'

'Any thoughts about where the treasure might be buried?'

Sponge sighed.

'Nothing, I'm afraid,' he replied.

'Maybe we should start trying to think like a pirate.'

'Intriguing,' said Sponge. 'What kind of a pirate am I?'

'Does that matter? A pirate. A generic pirate.'

Sponge thought for a while.

'Anything yet?' said Mildew hopefully.

Sponge thought for a few minutes and finally, heaving a great sigh of exhaustion, shook his head.

'I'm still trying to imagine what hat I would wear,' said Sponge.

'Hat?' said Mildew. 'What difference does a hat make, Sponge?'

'I have to think myself into the role,' said Sponge.

Mildew sighed and shook his head. Sponge groaned and slumped down on to the stone steps of the cloisters in a heap.

'Oh, it could be anywhere, Mildew,' said Sponge. 'And we don't even know if it is in Maudlin Towers. It could be at the top of Pug's Peak for all we know. Or in the bowels of Maudlin Mine.'

'True again,' said Mildew. 'But we must think of something, old friend. The whole school is depending on us. The future of Maudlin Towers is at stake!'

Sponge was suddenly struck by the notion that someone was watching him and looked around, half expecting to see Kenningworth skulking somewhere nearby.

Instead of which he was amazed to see a parrot sitting in a window just above their heads. It was bright green and, more remarkably still, wore an eyepatch over one eye. It fixed its remaining beady eye on Sponge in the most alarming manner.

'Look!' cried Sponge.

Mildew followed Sponge's gaze but saw only an empty window. 'What?'

'There was a parrot, Mildew,' said Sponge. 'A green parrot. With an eyepatch.'

Mildew peered at him.

'I wonder whether we ought to take you to see Nurse Leecham. I think that bump on the head may have broken your brain slightly.'

'It was there!' cried Sponge. 'I swear it.'

Plummeting Gargoyle

Mildew and Sponge were still arguing about the existence of the one-eyed parrot when they saw the Headmaster standing in the corridor outside his office beside a boy they did not recognise. He was a timid-looking chap, slim and pale, his hair black and neatly parted.

'Ah, boys,' said the Headmaster, smiling as they walked towards him. 'As you are here, perhaps I can call on you to befriend our new arrival and show him a warm Maudlin Towers welcome.'

Mildew and Sponge exchanged a glance of surprise that the Headmaster would accept new pupils when the school was in imminent danger of closure.

'Of course, sir,' said Mildew.

'Absolutely, sir,' said Sponge.

'If I could speak to you in private for a moment, boys.'

They left the new boy standing outside while the Headmaster brought them into his office and dropped his voice to a whisper.

'I can see that you think it strange that I should accept a new boy into the school at a time like this, but I assure you I did everything I could to put his guardian off.'

'His guardian?' said Sponge.

'Yes – the poor chap is an orphan,' said the Headmaster. 'But his parents left him very well provided for. Apparently it was a provision of their will that the boy be sent here. The guardian – a Mrs Daffowlille – insisted that whatever issues there were at the school, the boy should attend for as long as possible, even if that only turned out to be a matter of days. And, more to the point, she paid for the whole term up front. Every little helps, my boys.'

Mildew and Sponge nodded their agreement and the Headmaster led them back outside to where the new boy was patiently waiting.

'I'll leave you to it,' said the Headmaster, retreating into his office.

'What's your name?' asked Mildew of the new boy.

'Newboy,' said the new boy.

'No,' said Sponge. 'Your actual name.'

'My name is Newboy,' said the new boy.

'Your name is Newboy?' asked Mildew.

'And you are a new boy?' said Sponge.

New boy Newboy shrugged.

'An odd coincidence, I grant you,' he said. 'But there we are.'

'We'll look after you, won't we, Mildew?' said Sponge.

'Of course we will,' said Mildew. 'You couldn't have two better guides to Maudlin Towers.'

'Thank you,' said Newboy, clearly a little overcome. 'It's awfully frightening starting a new school.'

Mildew and Sponge nodded solemnly.

'I remember my first day,' said Sponge. 'I thought to myself that I'd never been to a place so horrible and uninviting, so cold and grim, so utterly without any redeeming features.'

'And now?' said Newboy brightly.

'Oh, I still think that,' said Sponge. 'Every day. Every single day.'

'Me too,' said Mildew.

Newboy's bottom lip began to quiver.

'Now, now,' said Mildew, patting him on the shoulder. 'You'll be all right. Won't he, Sponge?'

Sponge gave a non-committal shrug.

'Let's take you on a tour of the school,' said Mildew. 'Be brave. It's a soul-destroying business, but it has to be done.'

Newboy gulped.

'Where shall we start?' said Sponge.

'Well, you've met our glorious Headmaster,' said Mildew, placing his arm around Newboy's shoulder. 'He's as mad as a trouser full of wasps and has a smile that could stop a charging rhino, but as long as you stay out of his way he's relatively harmless.'

Newboy looked a little tearful.

'You've met Miss Pernickety, the school secretary, as well,' said Sponge breezily. 'She's not so bad.'

'Yes,' said Mildew. 'But never assume she has a sense of humour. Sponge made that mistake once, didn't you?'

Sponge shuddered at the recollection, and the boys led the increasingly troubled-looking Newboy towards the quad. Mildew looked up and Newboy followed his gaze.

'Maudlin Towers has four towers,' said Mildew, pointing his finger tower-wards. 'The Teetering Tower, the Tottering Tower, the Reasonably Stable Tower and the Trembling Tower. The Trembling Tower is that one with the clock face on it and it houses Big Brian, the largest of the school bells. You will never get used to its terrible tolling. Be warned.'

Right on cue, Big Brian struck the hour and the whole school shook to its foundations. A gargoyle from somewhere high above them plummeted to the ground, nose first, almost braining Newboy in the process.

'Any regrets at all about choosing Maudlin Towers?' said Mildew.

'One or two,' said Newboy faintly, staring at the grimacing gargoyle.

'Perhaps we ought to introduce him to some of the boys,' said Sponge with an encouraging smile.

'Agreed,' said Mildew. 'He's going to have to meet them eventually. Come along, Newboy.'

They turned the corner to find the boys sitting in their usual place. Kenningworth was holding court. They pointed out Enderpenny, Hipflask, Footstool, Furthermore and Filbert.

'That sharp-nosed, cactus-haired cove blathering like a walrus is Kenningworth,' said Mildew. 'Have nothing to do with him.'

'Yes,' agreed Sponge. 'He is a famous blot.'

'More to the point, it was he who released news of the school's secrets to the press. He thinks of no one but himself.'

They wandered over just as Kenningworth was finishing his story, to much eye-rolling from Furthermore.

'Ah,' said Kenningworth. 'Who's this?'

'He's new,' said Sponge. 'We're looking after him.'

'New, eh?' said Kenningworth. 'What's your name?'

'He's called Newboy,' said Mildew.

'Newboy?' said Kenningworth. 'But –'

'It's a coincidence,' said Sponge.

'Why on earth are you hanging out with these hairballs? Kenningworth's the name. Come on – I'll give you the tour.'

'We've already done that,' said Mildew.

'Ha!' said Kenningworth. 'They couldn't give you a tour of their own stupid faces.'

'That doesn't even make sense,' said Sponge.

Kenningworth waved the objection away and, to Mildew and Sponge's astonishment, Newboy walked away with Kenningworth without so much as a backward glance in their direction.

'Well, of all the …'

'Don't be too harsh on him, Mildew,' said Sponge. 'He's new.'

'Even so,' said Mildew. 'I feel let down.'

Sponge noticed a flash of green out of the corner of his eye.

'It's that parrot again,' said Sponge.

Mildew looked but the bird had flown.

'It was there!' said Sponge in answer to Mildew's sceptical glance.

'Seriously, Sponge,' said Mildew, 'I'm worried about you. I had a cousin who thought he could see Charles Dickens. It turned out to be a hatstand. He's a Member of Parliament now, Sponge. Be warned.'

'This was not an imaginary parrot,' said Sponge. 'It was there. I know it was. I saw it just as clearly as I can see you now.'

But Mildew had already walked away.

Miss Bronteen Tells All

reak over, Mildew and Sponge headed off
to their English lesson. As they entered
Miss Bronteen's classroom, they noticed
that Newboy was sitting next to Kenningworth.
He waved when he saw them. Sponge waved
back. Mildew scowled. Kenningworth scowled
back.

As usual Miss Bronteen stood looking out of
the window at the wind-and-rain-slapped Maudlin
Moors.

'Today,' she said without turning round, 'we shall
be looking at the work of the Gloomy Poets ...'

'Not the Gloomy Poets again,' whispered Mildew
as they took their places.

'Stop carping, Mildew,' hissed Kenningworth.

'Take out your books and turn to page 178.

Perhaps you might begin, Master Spongely-Partwork?'

Sponge dreaded reading out loud in class. He became so flustered he could barely hold the book, and Mildew had to find the right place for him. The pages shook so much in his hand he found it hard to read the words.

'An … An … An "Ode to Misery",' read Sponge tremulously, 'by Lord D'Spaire.'

Sponge coughed and puffed out his chest, ready to begin.

'O *Misery*, O –'

'Miss,' interrupted Newboy. 'Why is it that you look out of the window towards Maudlin Moor?'

There was a collective gasp from the boys. No one had ever asked Miss Bronteen why she did that. There was a general understanding that it would not be a good idea.

An almost imperceptible spasm jolted Miss Bronteen on hearing these words and, after what seemed an age, she turned round to face the boys.

'What is your name?' asked Miss Bronteen.

'Newboy,' said Newboy.

'Do you know,' said Miss Bronteen with a crooked smile, 'no one has ever asked me that question. Not in all these long years.'

'Yes,' said Kenningworth, frowning at Newboy. 'But he's new. He doesn't under–'

'No,' said Miss Bronteen with a sigh. 'Hush now, Kenningworth. I think I'd like to tell you. If you'd like to hear.'

The boys said they absolutely would. Anything to avoid another bout of the Gloomy Poets.

Miss Bronteen walked across the classroom in front of the boys and sat at her desk. She stared down for a long time before gazing out at them, tears sparkling in her dark eyes.

'It all began when I was a young woman with my whole life ahead of me. As carefree as a trout …

'I don't suppose you know that I am a local girl.'

The boys looked at each other. They knew nothing at all about her. They knew almost nothing about any of their teachers. Teachers were just teachers. Who knew how they came about. One might as well ponder the existence of nose hair.

63

'That's right. I hail from Lower Maudlin,' she continued, 'just a few miles down the road. As a girl I would roam the moors and the marshes, composing rambling rhymes as I rambled and roamed.

'Rain or hail, I cared not. I knew every rock and stream – every sheep dropping – by heart.

'Then, one fateful day, I saw him. He came riding towards me out of the mist on a coal-black steed. The horse reared up, startled at my presence, and threw the rider to the ground, where he lay stunned.

'I ran to his aid, calmed the horse and did my best to revive the fallen rider. After a moment or two, he regained his wits and stared up at me with eyes that seemed to look right at my very face.

'He told me that his family were sheep farmers. Their sheep had slobbered the slopes of Pug's Peak for centuries. I could see straight away that though he was rough and uneducated and incredibly handsome, he had a down-to-earth honesty about him that the preening fops my father wanted me to marry could never hope for.

'We fell in love there and then and vowed that we would always be together.'

Miss Bronteen faltered at this point and wiped a tear away. Mildew and Sponge studied their shoelaces.

'But one day,' continued Miss Bronteen, 'I arrived at our meeting place and he was not there. I waited and waited, though the weather was terrible. Drizzle drizzled relentlessly. Drizzle upon drizzle. Drizzle, drizzle, drizzle. I was drenched to the seventh layer of my undergarments. Hours I waited. But he came not.

'Fearing that some terrible accident had befallen him, I sent word to his home, and was told that he had left – left for a life as an accountant, with no thought of returning. With seemingly no thought of me.

'Without him my life was meaningless. I could see no future for myself. None whatsoever. In total despair I gave up on life completely, sinking lower and lower until finally I became' – *sob* – 'a teacher.'

Miss Bronteen was convulsed by some hearty, nose-bugling sobbing, throwing herself across her desk and moaning like a depressed whale.

'Sometimes …' she continued after a few moments, when she had composed herself. 'Sometimes, when I look out at the moors – when the weather is particularly foul – I imagine I see him still. And so I keep this vigil, despite knowing in my heart it is foolish.'

Miss Bronteen stood up and wandered across to

the window, turning her back on the boys once again. It was as though her revelation had never taken place. She was as she had always been.

'Men are vile, untrustworthy fellows,' she intoned morosely. 'Repeat ...'

'Men are vile, untrustworthy fellows,' repeated the class.

'Excellent,' said Miss Bronteen. 'Keep saying that until the bell.'

A Letter from the Governors

Mildew and Sponge left the class with the other boys and headed off to their next lesson.

'I wonder if Miss Bronteen will ever find her true love again?' asked Sponge. 'I felt my heart-strings well and truly plucked, I don't mind saying.'

'What's got into you, Sponge?' said Mildew. 'You sound like a poet.'

'Sorry,' said Sponge sheepishly. 'I don't know what came over me.'

'I'm more concerned about Newboy being led astray by Kenn–'

At that moment, the Headmaster appeared at the door of his office, grabbed Mildew and Sponge by the scruff of their necks and dragged them inside, slamming the door shut. He pointed to a letter in his hand.

'It's hopeless,' said the Headmaster, even his fixed smile wobbling a little. 'Look!'

The Headmaster showed them a letter.

Ahoy there Headmaster
Arrr! Be so good as to muster
all the staff and have them
assemble ~~on the poop deck~~
in the school hall afore
awaiting our instructions
Arrr!
Yours truly
Chair of Governors
PS Arrr

'It's an odd sort of letter, isn't it?' said Sponge. 'I would have imagined school governors to have a more refined way with words.'

'Sir Brashly Bugle is a former military man, as I told you,' said the Headmaster. 'They probably all speak like that in the army.'

'Well, sir,' said Sponge, 'my Aunt Bernard served in the Guards but she has a very delicate turn of phrase.'

'Be that as it may,' said the Headmaster, 'the fact remains that the governors are on their way and possibly armed. They could arrive at any moment. It's looking bleak for us all, boys. Bleak as Wednesday.'

Though the Headmaster's ever-present smile was still in place, the boys could see the troubled look in his eyes and a panicky twitch around the nostril region.

They left the Headmaster and were on their way to their next lesson, which was art with Mr Riddell, when Sponge realised he had forgotten his pencils and went off to fetch them from the dorm.

As Mildew waited for his friend he looked back and saw Kenningworth skulking about again near the Headmaster's office.

'What are you doing?' said Mildew. 'What's with all this lurking about, Kenningworth? What are you up to?'

'I can explain everything,' said Kenningworth, pulling a watch and chain from his pocket and waving it in front of Mildew's face, back and forth, back and forth.

'How exactly does a dangling watch explain anyth–'

Mildew found he no longer had the will to talk and instead had an irresistible urge to follow the shiny pocket watch with his eyes.

'You are in my power,' said Kenningworth.

'I am in your power,' said Mildew.

'Where is the treasure?' said Kenningworth.

'Where is the treasure?' said Mildew.

'Don't just repeat everything I say, you fool.'

'Don't just repeat ev–'

'Tell me where the treasure is!' demanded Kenningworth.

'We don't know,' said Mildew.

Kenningworth groaned.

'What are you and Sponge up to, then?'

'Sponge saw a clue on the sail of the ship in a bottle but he got hit on the head and can't remember it.'

'Grrr,' said Kenningworth. 'When I say the word "balloon" you will forget everything that happened in the last ten minutes.'

'Forget everything that happened,' repeated Mildew.

'Balloon,' said Kenningworth.

Mildew shook his head and peered at Kenningworth.

'Kenningworth,' he said. 'What are you doing here?'

'I was just asking you the same thing,' said Kenningworth. 'Don't you remember?'

'Not really, no,' said Mildew. 'What did I reply?'

'You were looking for the Headmaster, apparently.'

'Was I?' said Mildew. 'What were you doing?'

'I was looking for him too,' said Kenningworth. 'As you can see, he's not here.'

Mildew walked away towards a returning Sponge, still trying to shake off a slight dizzy feeling in his head.

'Hello, Sponge,' he said. 'Where have you been?'

'Back to the dorm to get my pencils, of course,' said Sponge, peering at him. 'What were you talking to Kenningworth about and why was he showing you his watch?'

'His watch?' said Mildew. 'What ever do you mean?'

'I mean his watch,' said Sponge. 'He dangled it in front of your face. I saw him.'

'No dangling occurred whatsoever, Sponge,' said Mildew. 'You're seeing things. Again. Are you sure it wasn't a parrot he was dangling?'

Mildew chuckled to himself. Sponge did not.

'It was a watch!' said Sponge, scowling. 'And the parrot was real! Did you ask Kenningworth what he was up to?'

'We were both looking for the Headmaster.'

'No, you weren't,' said Sponge. 'You were waiting for me. For some reason you headed off to talk to Kenningworth. I saw you. Then he waggled his watch.'

'I think I know what was and wasn't waggled, Sponge,' said Mildew.

'Well, we can't both be right,' said Sponge.

'Thank you,' said Mildew. 'I accept your apology. Let us say no more about it.'

Sponge opened his mouth but no words presented themselves and he closed it once more. The bell rang and off they went to their art lesson.

The Mystery of the Man on the Moor

Mr Riddell had placed a sheet of paper in front of each boy.

'Very well,' he said. 'You have thirty minutes. I want you to draw the dark recesses of your innermost soul.'

'Not again,' grumbled Mildew.

'Make sure you write your name clearly at the bottom of your work. I want to know whose soul I'm looking at. Begin!'

Afterwards, each one now questioning the very meaning of his own existence, the boys wandered into the school grounds in search of some air to clear their heads.

'Look,' said Sponge, pointing into the distance.

'What at?' said Mildew.

'There,' said Sponge, pointing. 'On the moors.

A man standing on that outcrop, bedraggled and bedrizzled.'

The boys gasped as the image became fractionally clearer. Sure enough, the fuzzy shape of a man was just visible, standing on a rocky outcrop.

'Yes,' said Mildew, squinting. 'Just as Miss Bronteen described in her sorry tale.'

The two boys looked at each other in wonder.

'It's not another ghost, is it?' said Sponge.

'To be fair, if you're referring to the Viking in the ha-ha or Enderpenny's ghost in the attic, they weren't actually ghosts, were they? So if this one is, it would be a first.'

The drizzle intensified and the figure melted into it and was gone. The two boys gasped again.

'It's all very mysterious, Mildew,' said Sponge.

'But have we got time for another mystery, Sponge? We need to save the school,' said Mildew. 'The Mystery of the Man on Maudlin Moor may have to wait.'

'But shouldn't we tell Miss Bronteen?'

'Tell her what, Sponge?' said Mildew. 'That we saw a vague and distant silhouette of a man in the drizzle? I don't think we should test her emotions further. Emotions are dangerous things. My father has been a martyr to them.'

'But –' butted Sponge.

'Mildew! Sponge!' hissed someone unseen.

The boys turned at the sound but could see no one.

'Over here!' came the hissed voice.

It was Newboy, peeping round a doorway under one of the buttresses.

He gestured for them to come closer.

'In here,' he said, and they followed him through the doorway.

'Where's your new friend Kenningworth?' said Mildew.

'Kenningworth isn't my friend,' said Newboy. 'You were right about him. I was spying. It's true. He's up to something.'

'Kenningworth's always up to something,' said Mildew.

'I saw him dangling a watch in front of Mildew's face,' said Sponge. 'And then –'

'Don't listen to him,' said Mildew. 'He has suffered a severe thud to the head. His judgement is impaired.'

'No, it isn't,' protested Sponge.

'It is,' said Mildew. 'He's been seeing parrots.'

Sponge opened his mouth to defend himself but Newboy spoke first.

'Kenningworth's after the treasure too.'

'What?' said Mildew. 'For himself?'

Newboy nodded.

'He wants the money, but he also wants to stop the Headmaster having the means to save the school. He told me so himself.'

'He's even worse than I suspected,' said Sponge.

'I thought if I won his trust then I could keep an eye on him and report back to you,' said Newboy.

'Excellent idea,' said Mildew.

Newboy smiled and walked away. Mildew watched him leave and turned to Sponge.

'What a good sort Newboy is,' said Mildew.

'Agreed,' said Sponge. 'I hope we become firm friends.'

'Yes,' said Mildew. 'Although we will always be Mildew and Sponge, Sponge.'

Sponge smiled.

'He can be our second-best friend, Mildew.'

'I think he is a very worthy candidate for that position, Sponge. You were wrong to doubt him.'

'What?' said Sponge. 'Me? But –'

'Shh now, Sponge,' said Mildew. 'Don't spoil the moment.'

Mildew and Sponge were on their way to lunch when they heard a strange squeaking noise. They turned to see a tall, cloaked and hooded figure in a three-cornered hat gliding towards them down the corridor, rainwater dripping from his clothes. A group of other similarly attired figures followed in his wake.

'Aaargh!' squeaked Mildew and Sponge.

'Arrr!' replied the figure as he drew close and removed his hat.

His face remained beshadowed by his hood but they could see he had a large beard and long black hair – and a pair of gold hooped earrings. Two great pistols and a cutlass hung from his wide leather belt, the buckle of which was fashioned in the

shape of the Maudlin Towers school badge: a winged and grinning skull.

The stranger's left leg was missing below the knee and replaced by a wooden shaft that was socketed into a horizontal plank with wheels underneath it at either end. The stranger followed their inquisitive gaze.

'Be ye looking at my leg?' asked the man.

'No,' said Sponge. 'That is … I … well …'

'Arrr. Not very polite, is it,' he said, 'to stare at another man's misfortune?'

'I wasn't,' said Sponge. 'I was looking at … the … er … wood. I like wood. Don't I, Mildew?'

'Oh yes,' said Mildew. 'He can't get enough of it. He's wood-mad.'

'Arrr,' said the man. 'I had the rest of me leg took clean off by a morose turtle. Just off the straits of Malacca.'

'Sounds painful,' said Mildew. 'I once trapped my toe in the door and it hurt for days.'

The stranger stared at him.

'Yours was probably worse though,' said Mildew. 'Erm … interesting thingamajig.'

Mildew pointed to the thingamajig.

'Arrr! This here contraption be an ingenious device of me own devising,' said the stranger. 'It be some compensation for my loss of mobility, allowing me to scoot along in a most satisfying fashion, as you have just observed. I calls it me patented wooden leg mobility facilitator.'

'Not "scooter"?' suggested Mildew.

The stranger peered at him.

'Scooter, eh?' he said, stroking his beard. 'Arrr! That is better, come to think of it.'

'Can we be of assistance in any way?' said Sponge.

'Arrr!' said the man, as though suddenly remembering his original purpose. 'Did I not announce myself? We be the school governors.'

The group behind muttered a set of rather menacing 'arrr's and 'aye's.

Mildew and Sponge took a step backward.

'I be the Captain – I mean *Chair* of Governors. Where be the Headmaster of this establishment?'

'Maybe he is getting the staff together in the hall,' said Mildew. 'As you requested in your letter.'

'How do you know about the letter?' growled the Chair of Governors, looming over Mildew. Sponge whimpered.

'The Headmaster showed it to us,' he said.

'Did he now?' said the Chair of Governors, peering at them. 'Interesting. What say you two shrimps scuttle off and tell the Headmaster we've arrived?'

With that, the Chair of Governors gave himself a push with his right leg and then stepped aboard the wheeled plank to scoot down the corridor towards the hall, squeaking into the distance. The other cloaked and hooded figures followed and the hall door slammed shut behind them.

'They were very odd, weren't they?' said Mildew as they walked to the Headmaster's office.

'Perhaps,' said Sponge. 'I've never met any governors before. I've heard some are very odd indeed.'

'Yes. I wonder which one was Kenningworth's mother?'

'Sir,' said Mildew, on seeing the Headmaster walking towards them. 'I'm afraid the governors are here.'

The Headmaster sighed.

'Well, I suppose it was inevitable,' he replied. 'I shall gather the staff together and we will endeavour to state our case – that Maudlin Towers is too important an institution to be allowed simply to die.'

The Headmaster walked away.

'Is this the end of Maudlin Towers, Mildew?' said Sponge.

'I fear it may be,' said Mildew.

'But I don't want to be sent to another school,'

said Sponge. 'Maudlin Towers is cold and depress-
ing – but so are lots of things.'

'Agreed, old friend,' said Mildew. 'Many of those
things are relatives. But we must try to be brave.'

They tried to be brave for a minute or so, but
both agreed it was far too exhausting.

11 Another Crumbling Pinnacle

The Headmaster rounded up all the staff and they plodded off to the hall like prisoners going to the gallows. Mildew and Sponge stood with the other boys watching them go. Even the hardest of hearts was softened at the sight.

'What's going on?' said Furthermore.

'The governors have arrived,' said Sponge. 'They are having a meeting with the Headmaster and all the staff.'

'The governors?' said Kenningworth nervously. 'What? My mother's here?'

He quickly began to tidy himself up, straightening his tie and sharpening the points of his hair.

'What do the governors want?' said Enderpenny.

'I'm afraid the Headmaster has asked us to keep that in confidence,' said Mildew.

'They're here to close this dump down,' said Kenningworth.

'What?!' cried the boys.

'It's true,' said Kenningworth. 'And they know it too.'

He pointed to Mildew and Sponge, who after a while could think of nothing to do except nod in agreement.

'He's right,' said Mildew, frowning at Kenningworth. 'The school does appear to be doomed.'

'But why?' said Newboy plaintively. 'I've only just got here.'

'The new Chair of Governors thinks this place is too soft,' said Mildew. 'That's why the teachers look so glum. It's hard to imagine who else would employ some of them.'

The boys all underwent the same sequence of emotions as Mildew and Sponge: their shock gave way to rapture, and then, as it dawned on them that they might be separated from their chums and sent to who-knew-where, a despondency not unlike that they had seen shrouding the staff descended upon them too. All apart from Kenningworth …

'Oh, buck up, you lot,' he said. 'It's not as though it's the end of the world, is it?'

'It's all right for him,' said Mildew. 'His mother is going to send him off to some soft school in the south of France.'

The boys all turned to face Kenningworth, a scowl on every face. He sniffed and raised an eyebrow, seeing that this revelation had not been well received.

'That is just one of the possibilities under consideration,' he said. 'I refuse to feel bad about it. Anywhere has to be better than this frightful place. Don't pretend you like it here any more than I do.'

No one could think of a suitable response to this,

and Mildew and Sponge's young brains were still boggled by the arrival of the strange governors as they walked across the quad, eager to get away from Kenningworth. Just then, another crumbling pinnacle decided to break loose and plummet earthward.

It crashed into a parapet thirty feet below, where most of it remained, the other third or so bouncing on to a roof ridge and smashing into smaller pieces that rained down into the gutter – all except one piece, which escaped to hit the top of a buttress and shatter into even smaller fragments, the largest of which – no bigger than the beak of a small duck – hit Sponge on the top of his bristly head, knocking him senseless.

'Sponge!' said Mildew, picking his friend up and shaking him.

When he received no response, he slapped Sponge round the face.

'Ow!' said Sponge. 'That hurt.'

'I was worried,' said Mildew.

'Remind me to slap you round the face the next time I'm worried about you,' said Sponge, rubbing his face with one hand and the bump that was emerging on his head with the other. 'I'm sure that hit me in exactly the same place as the – wait! I remember!'

'You remember what it said on the sail?' said Mildew.

'I do!' said Sponge. 'It said: I *am at sea among the dead.*'

Mildew frowned. Sponge gave his bump another prod and winced. Looking up, he saw the green parrot with the eyepatch perched on a nearby buttress.

'There it is again!' shouted Sponge, pointing.

But again, the parrot had disappeared by the time Mildew looked round.

'Now will you accept there is a direct link between you getting bumped on the head and the glimpsing of parrots?' said Mildew, shaking his head.

'It was there,' said Sponge. 'I know it was.'

But even he was starting to have doubts.

'At *sea among the dead,*' said Mildew, returning to Sponge's flash of memory. 'What "dead" do you think?'

'The graveyard,' said Sponge after a moment. 'Maybe the treasure is in the graveyard?'

Mildew nodded.

'Good thinking, Sponge. Very good thinking.'

Sponge smiled and blushed.

'Thank you, Mildew,' he said. 'My brain just seemed to work all of a sudden.'

'Odd how that can happen,' said Mildew. 'If only one could control it somehow.'

The two boys headed off towards the staff graveyard, picking their way through the headstones until they came to a halt beside Mr Particle's gravestone. It showed a winged hourglass.

'I'm glad they moved old Particle into the staff cemetery,' said Sponge, looking at their old physics teacher's headstone.

'Yes – although if the Headmaster and Flintlock hadn't panicked and buried him in the grounds, they wouldn't have found that Roman bust of you, Sponge.'

'True,' said Sponge.

'And it's nice you don't bear Particle any ill will at all, despite him trying to kill you.'

'He wasn't himself, Mildew,' said Sponge. 'And besides – he tried to kill both of us, not just me.'

'True,' agreed Mildew. 'Very true.'

'Do you think the money really was still in the chair-turned-time-machine when it travelled back to the age of dinosaurs?' said Sponge.

'I fear it must have been, Sponge,' said Mildew. 'Surely old Particle would have scarpered if he'd found it. Why stay here if you had all that loot?'

'Agreed,' said Sponge. 'And it won't do Mr Stupendo much good, will it? I don't suppose they had biscuit shops in dinosaur times.'

'Probably not,' agreed Mildew, not rising to Sponge's biscuit bait. 'It's a crying shame, that's for sure. All that money wasted.'

'What are we going to do, Mildew?' said Sponge. 'I don't want to go to another school. Not without you. I'd even miss Enderpenny, Hipflask, Filbert and Furthermore.'

'I know,' said Mildew. 'But the money is gone for good. The only way to save the school is to find the treasure!'

'But how?' said Sponge. 'The treasure could be anywhere in Maudlin Towers or its grounds. Where would we start?'

Mildew flapped his hand about as though swatting a family of gnats.

'Pish, Sponge,' he said. 'Didn't we solve the mystery of the Curse of the Werewolf Boy?'

'In a way,' said Sponge doubtfully. 'I suppose.'

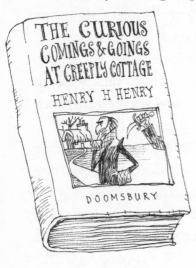

'Exactly!' cried Mildew triumphantly. 'We must be detectives once more! Remember *The Curious Comings and Goings at Creeply Cottage*, the latest Henry H. Henry book I was showing you last week? What would the great detective Finlay Feathering do at a time like this?'

Both boys instinctively raised a hand to their chins, as Mildew's hero was depicted doing on the cover.

'He might ... eat some biscuits,' said Sponge after a moment.

'I'm not sure he –'

'I need some food, Mildew. My brain is hungry,' said Sponge. 'A biscuit wouldn't go amiss at a time like this.'

'Yes – well, there are no biscuits, Sponge. As I said.'

Sponge peered at him sceptically.

'Not actually here,' said Sponge. 'Not in this graveyard, no …'

Mildew glared at him.

'Your head is full of biscuits. Buck up, Sponge. How are you ever going to detectivate? Finlay Feathering wouldn't let a bit of biscuitlessness bother him.'

Sponge crossed his arms in a fashion he had seen employed by his Aunt Bernard when dealing with troublesome tradesmen. Mildew seemed impervious. Sponge looked away, muttering.

'Wait a minute,' said Mildew. 'We're looking in the wrong place. This graveyard wouldn't have been here in Greenbeard's time. This one's full of teacherly ribs and funny bones. We need to look in the Old Graveyard – the family plot of the ancient Maudlins.'

'N-N-Not the Old G-G-Graveyard?' said Sponge tremulously.

None of the boys ever entered the Old Graveyard, the ancient, dank and wormy resting place of the

Maudlin family, stuffed full of crumbling old tombs and dusty vaults.

'We won't be in there long,' said Mildew. 'Come on.'

Reluctantly, Sponge followed his friend through the rusting, ivy-clad gates to the Maudlin family graveyard. The day was dark and overcast and added to the place's natural gothic grimness. They walked through its cobbled, cobwebbed alleyways and stared at the rows of family mausoleums and monumental headstones.

'Look,' said Sponge. 'That grave over there.'

Sponge pointed to a particular headstone, blackened like all the others, with green mould glowing among its various nooks and crevices, but much less grand. More importantly, it had a winged skull and three-masted ship sailing on a storm-tossed sea engraved into the stone.

'The *Golden Skull!*' they cried.

'Look at the inscription,' said Sponge. 'It says he lived on Mute Row Island. The same anagram-matical island that the treasure was supposedly buried on.'

'You're right, Sponge,' said Mildew. 'Maybe the treasure is buried right here!'

Sponge leaned forward, looking at the headstone.

'There's something odd here,' he said. 'A thin piece of plaster – and there's writing behind it …'

Sponge picked at the plaster and it fell off in one piece.

'Sponge!' cried Mildew. 'Will you stop breaking things!'

But the boys saw now that the sheet of plaster had been covering up another inscription. It read:

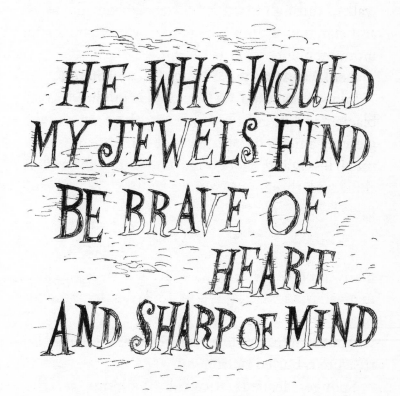

HE WHO WOULD
MY JEWELS FIND
BE BRAVE OF
HEART
AND SHARP OF MIND

And then, a little further down:

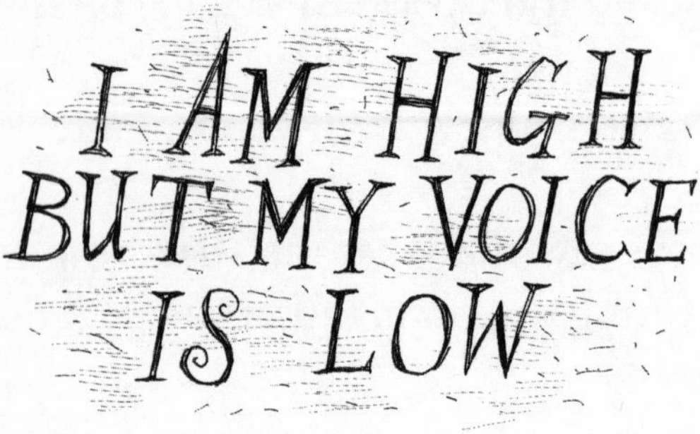

I AM HIGH
BUT MY VOICE
IS LOW

'But what can that possibly mean?' said Sponge.
'I have absolutely no idea,' said Mildew.

An Inquisitive Child's Guide to Hypnotism

ildew and Sponge wandered back into the school, turning the clue over and over in their minds, but a solution refused to occur to them. What was high and had a low voice? It seemed a meaningless riddle.

They passed Kenningworth as they walked through the entrance hall. He ignored them both and seemed utterly engrossed in studying his pocket watch. Mildew came to a halt, staring not at Kenningworth but at Kenningworth's watch. Sponge pulled him away. Mildew shook his head, dazed, as though coming out of a deep sleep.

'Come to the library, Mildew,' said Sponge, casting a scowl in the direction of Kenningworth. 'I've got something to show you.'

Mildew tried to ask him what and why, but Sponge

darted off with a surprising turn of speed and by the time Mildew caught up, Sponge was already in their usual corner of the library, book on lap.

'Look,' said Sponge as Mildew sat down. 'See. It explains everything.'

Mildew looked at the book. It was called *An Inquisitive Child's Guide to Hypnotism*.

'Sponge,' he cried. 'For once and for all, I have not been hypnotised.'

'But look,' said Sponge. 'That's the whole thing about hypnotism. The person doesn't know they've been hypnotised. They can make you forget. You see?'

Mildew heaved a sigh, but read the passage Sponge pointed out. There was an illustration of a fiendish-looking character dangling a watch in front of his hapless victim, who stared on impassively.

'Wait!' hissed Mildew. 'Do you know, I think you're on to something, Sponge. I had a flash of memory then.'

Sponge opened the book at the front and showed the list of recent borrowers. There was a name they recognised halfway up.

'Kenningworth!' they cried.

Mildew and Sponge found Kenningworth and the others were waiting for news from the meeting of staff and governors.

'See here, Kenningworth,' said Sponge, 'why did you hypnotise Mildew?'

Enderpenny and the others crowded round to hear what the fuss was.

'Hypnotise Mildew?' said Hipflask. 'What's this?'

'They are making it up,' said Kenningworth.

'Don't try to lie,' said Mildew. 'We know you took a book on hypnotism out of the library before the half-term hols.'

'I know,' said Kenningworth with a shrug. 'So? I thought it might be fun to try to hypnotise Mr Painly into forgetting about my homework. It didn't work.'

'Don't you think it's a coincidence that I see you dangling a watch in front of Mildew's face a few weeks later?'

'It would be,' said Kenningworth. 'Had I so dangled.'

'Pah!' said Mildew.

'I saw you with my own eyes,' said Sponge, pointing at Kenningworth. 'You hypnotised Mildew.'

'I'd rather hypnotise my own foot,' said Kenningworth.

Mildew and Sponge exchanged puzzled glances and shrugged.

'It's gone very quiet in there,' said Newboy, looking back towards the hall.

The boys all followed his gaze. Newboy was right: it was very quiet. They looked at each other then slowly edged their way hall-ward, straining to hear. Their ears were about to touch the door when it was suddenly yanked open and they tumbled through, Sponge luckily softening their fall.

When the boys got to their feet they noticed two puzzling things: a total absence of their teachers and a strange burning smell. Glancing around, they saw a large burnt patch on the rug.

The rather unfriendly-looking stranger who had opened the door grunted at Hipflask to fetch the rest of the pupils, and he ran off to do so. Mildew, Sponge and the others stood in worried silence.

It seemed an age before a rumble of footsteps

signalled the return of Hipflask, the rest of the school in his wake. Soon the hall was full and the boys waited to discover the meaning of what they were all staring at.

On the stage was a very strange collection of people.

Strange in the sense they were odd, but also strange in the sense that they were strangers and the boys had no idea who they were. The tallest of them glided forward to the gasps of the assembled children and, after holding up his hands for silence, began to speak.

'Arrr,' he said. 'Ye may be wonderin' who I be.'

A puzzled silence gripped the room.

'I be your new Headmaster,' he continued.

The silence was broken by a buzz of confused jabbering.

'He be the new Headmaster,' whispered Sponge.

'Why are you talking like that, Sponge?' said Mildew.

'He started it. I be just –'

'He looks an awful lot like the Chair of Governors,' said Mildew. 'Look at his leg. Or his lack of leg.'

Sponge looked, and sure enough, the new Headmaster had the same wooden scooter-for-a-leg device. He glided across the stage as he spoke. And there was something else …

'Look,' said Sponge. 'There's that one-eyed green parrot I've been seeing. Sitting on the Headmaster's shoulder.'

'So there was a parrot!' said Mildew. 'I was wrong to doubt you, Sp–'

'Silence!' roared the new Headmaster, scooting forward to the edge of the stage. 'Arrr! Stow your blather, ye mangy dogs, or I'll have ye swabbing the poop!'

Silence returned – apart from a faint and mysterious thudding noise.

'Arrr. That's better. Now ye may be wonderin' why ye have a new Headmaster at all. Which brings me to some awful sad news.'

Mildew noted that the new Headmaster did not look awful sad.

'I'm afraid a terrible occurrence has occurred. Arrr. The entire gaggle of teachers has spontaneously combusted. Aye. Burnt to a crisp, every man jack of 'em. Terrible thing to be sure, but there we are. We must all move on.'

The boys looked on, wide-eyed and wide-mouthed.

'What's spontaneous combustion?' whispered Sponge.

'It's when someone goes up in flames, Sponge,' said Mildew.

'Like Joan of Arc?' said Sponge.

'Joan of Arc was tied to a stake standing on a pile of wood chips, Sponge. She was set alight with a flaming torch. This is when people burst into flame, but without the stake and chips.'

'Pipe down, Mildew,' said Kenningworth.

'The governors have asked us to come to the school as replacements,' said the replacement Headmaster.

'Sir,' said Newboy, to gasps. 'Where are the governors now?'

'Arrr – they had to leave. In a hurry. Things to do, apparently.'

'But, sir,' began Newboy again.

'Hush your jabber!' growled the replacement Headmaster. 'Everything will carry on as before so long as ye all do as you're told. Your boggle-eyed Reverend Brimstone will be replaced by our own boggle-eyed Preacher Bob.'

A huge man stepped forward, scars all over his face. Not quite as terrifying as Reverend Brimstone, but the front row of children took a step back just to be on the safe side. The replacement Headmaster grinned.

'Your new maths teacher will be Nevermiss Nellie …'

A bald-headed, copiously tattooed woman strode forward, fists on hips.

'Art will be taught by Charlie Two-Brushes …'

A paint-spattered man to her right scowled, a gold tooth twinkling.

'History will be taught by Mizzenmast Mary …'

A wild-haired woman shoved her way forward. Sponge gulped.

'French will be taught by Jacques Blacques …'

The replacement French teacher spat out the dagger he'd been clenching between his teeth and it hammered into the edge of the stage, making the boys at the front squeak. He smirked at the response.

'And English will be taught by Crow's-Nest Jake …'

A tall and handsome man came forward, nodded and waved at the assembled boys.

The Headmaster continued to introduce everyone on stage until they all stood in a line and every member of Maudlin staff had a replacement.

'Arrr,' continued the Headmaster, looking out at the worried faces. 'No need to concern yourselves. So long as ye all abide by my rules there'll be no need for anyone to be flogged, keel-hauled or marooned, now, will there?'

'What's keel-hauling?' whispered Sponge.

'It's a nautical punishment,' said Furthermore. 'They pull you from one side of the ship to the other, underwater, snagging you on the barnacles as they do so.'

Sponge whimpered again.

'I don't want my barnacles snagged,' said Sponge.

'It would smart, that's for sure,' said Mildew.

'What was that thudding noise when the Headmaster called for quiet?' Sponge asked.

'Didn't hear a thing,' said Kenningworth.

'Sorry, Sponge,' said Mildew. 'Me neither.'

Pirate Teachers

Mildew and Sponge joined Enderpenny, Hipflask and Furthermore in the cloisters.

'Can you believe it?' said Enderpenny.

'Can the staff really all be gone?' said Hipflask. 'Up in a puff of smoke?'

'It seems rather suspicious if you ask me,' said Furthermore.

'Oh, you think everything is suspicious,' said Kenningworth.

'And you don't?' said Furthermore. 'Didn't those replacement teachers look a bit odd to you?'

'Odd?' said Kenningworth. 'They're teachers. It's in their nature to be odd.'

'The whole staff suddenly combust and are replaced by this collection of growling grotesques?'

continued Furthermore. 'It all seems a bit odd. How did the governors leave without us seeing them?'

'It does seem odd,' said Sponge. 'Furthermore's right. Added to which, the new Headmaster looks awfully like the Chair of Governors.'

'He does, Sponge,' said Mildew.

'Perhaps they're brothers,' said Newboy.

'He looks nothing like the Chair of Governors,' said Kenningworth. 'My mother is a governor as you know. I met him last hols. He's also a fright – but in an entirely different way.'

'I beg to differ,' said Mildew. 'We met the Chair of Governors only very recently and they could be twins.'

'Maybe they are,' said Hipflask.

'I suppose they both have a leg missing?' said Furthermore. 'And zip about on that wheeled contraption.'

'Well, as a matter of fact …' said Mildew.

'Perhaps they are identical twins,' said Sponge.

'Yes,' said Mildew. 'I don't suppose you thought of that, did you, Kenningworth?'

Furthermore rolled his eyes.

'And why didn't your mother say hello?' said Mildew. 'Mothers never miss a chance to smother their offspring in hugging and such like.'

'That is a bit odd, come to think of it,' said

Kenningworth. 'Mumsy – I mean Mother – is normally very attentive. And why isn't she taking me away to my new school?'

'I'm telling you, something isn't right,' said Furthermore.

'What does any of it matter?' said Kenningworth. 'The school is going to get closed down – and, frankly, if staying open means it's going to be run by these oddballs, who cares?'

The boys grumbled and mumbled but the consensus was that Kenningworth, once again, had a point.

'I felt strange,' said Hipflask, 'when he told us about the teachers combusting. I can't quite explain it.'

'I know,' said Enderpenny. 'I felt odd as well.'

The rest of the boys nodded in agreement and all joined in, saying they too had felt a peculiar sensation on hearing the news.

'You don't think ...' began Furthermore but stopped, shaking his head as though the thought was preposterous.

'What?' said Mildew.

'Well,' he said, with a confused look on his face. 'You don't think we were ... sad?'

They all chuckled at this idea and Furthermore joined them. But the chuckling quickly faded and they stared back towards the hall door in confusion. Yes. Extraordinary as it seemed, they were sad.

Mildew noticed that Sponge kept opening his mouth to speak and then changing his mind and closing it – only to open it once again after a few seconds, and then close it again. The repetition of this action gave him the appearance of a beached haddock.

'What is it, Sponge?'

'Well,' said Sponge. 'I've been thinking.'

Mildew nodded sympathetically.

'We've talked about this before, haven't we?' said Mildew. 'It always makes you feel faint.'

'The replacement teachers,' said Sponge.

'What about them?' said Furthermore.

'Wait here,' said Sponge, and ran off, his tiny feet pattering away into the distance.

The boys waited for several minutes with much sighing and sniffing, until Sponge returned, gasping and carrying *Every Boy's Book of Pirates* under his arm.

He opened it and pointed to a page showing a group of pirates standing on the deck of their ship.

'You see?' said Sponge. 'The earrings, the eyepatches, the parrot – the tattoos that say "Pirates arrrr us" and "I be a pirate"? They aren't teachers at all!'

The boys gasped.

'No,' agreed Mildew. 'They be pirates – every man Jack of them.'

'Aye,' said Sponge.

'They must have been alerted by the newspaper article,' said Furthermore.

'Do pirates read newspapers?' asked Filbert.

'Clearly they do,' said Mildew.

'What a strange coincidence that the staff would all spontaneously combust just as they turn up, and the governors just leave,' said Hipflask.

'Don't you see?' said Furthermore. 'The governors were never here. They were the pirates too. As Mildew said, the Chair of Governors and the Pirate Headmaster are one and the same!'

'What about the Maudlin staff though?' said Sponge.

'The pirates must have done away with them somehow,' said Mildew.

'Done away with?' said Sponge dizzily. 'This story isn't going to involve b-b-b–'

'Soup?' said Mildew.

'Soup?' said Newboy.

'It's what we say instead of the "b" word for the red runny stuff,' explained Mildew.

Kenningworth shook his head.

'I'm afraid soup may very well have been on the menu, Sponge,' continued Mildew. 'I wouldn't put it past these black-hearted rogues. I suspect pirate hands are always a bit soupy.'

'Even your ancestor's?' sneered Kenningworth. 'Greenbeard?'

'I expect the Mildew code would have come out in him,' said Mildew defensively. 'Even as a pirate. I can't believe he was a Mildew and wholly bad. I just sense it somehow. It's in the soup.'

'But what did they do to everyone?' said Furthermore. 'Dead or alive, how did they make them disappear?'

'I don't know,' said Mildew. 'It's a mystery all right.'

Miss Nevermiss

*L*essons were abandoned for the rest of the day and the boys woke the following morning after a troubled night, anxious about what news the day might bring. They decided not to let on that they had seen through the pirates' ruse and wait to see what the intruders did next. The bell rang for the start of lessons and Mildew and Sponge headed off to maths with more than their usual air of dread and despondency. They filed in with the others and took their seats.

Instead of their teacher Mr Painly, whose whereabouts were as yet unknown, there was a woman – although this was initially hard to discern as she was dressed from head to foot in men's clothing, all topped with a teacher's gown.

'Arrr,' said their new maths teacher. 'I goes by the name of Nevermiss Nellie, but you can call me Miss Nevermiss. Any questions?'

'How are you spelling Nevermiss, miss?' asked Enderpenny.

'Arrr!' she said. 'N, E –'

'R, N, E …' repeated Enderpenny.

'No, you whelk!' she cried. 'No "R". Just N, E, V –'

'Just N, E, V …' repeated Enderpenny.

'Aye!' said Miss Nevermiss.

'N, E, V, I …' said Enderpenny.

Miss Nevermiss sighed and wrote her name on the blackboard.

'Anything else?' she said.

Newboy put his hand up.

'Why do they call you Nevermiss, miss?'

A look of terrifying seriousness came over Miss Nevermiss's face and she reached deep into the pockets of her trousers, bringing out first a huge knife and then a long-barrelled flintlock pistol. The boys gasped.

Miss Nevermiss put the gun and the knife on the table and rummaged around further, finding a piece of paper, which she screwed into a tight ball. She clicked her neck and, taking aim, threw the screwed-up ball into the waste-paper

bin on the other side of
the class.

'That,' she said
with a self-satisfied
grin, 'is why they call
me Nevermiss!'

The boys erupted
into applause.

Miss Nevermiss
scribbled furiously
on the blackboard
for a few moments
and then stepped back to reveal a complicated
diagram involving several ships, rowing
boats, islands, treasure chests, shark fins and
cannons.

'Arrr,' she said. 'You are the captain of a schooner.
You have thirty-two in your crew. You have just
taken possession of an American frigate loaded
with two hogsheads of gold dubloons, three sacks
of silver and a sea chest filled with jewels and pearls
and all manner of trinkets. How do we divide the
spoils between the crew?'

As usual, the boys emerged from their maths lesson
dizzy with brain-ache, although Sponge was aware
of a strange feeling.

'Mildew,' he said quietly as they shuffled down the corridor.

'Yes?' said Mildew.

'There was a point in the maths lesson where I had the peculiar sensation that I was actually understanding.'

Mildew stopped and stared at him.

'I know what ye mean,' said Mildew. 'Like suddenly seeing a Barbary galley appearing out of the mist?'

'Arrr,' said Sponge. 'Precisely.'

The boys then headed off to their English lesson.

'Arrr!' said Miss Bronteen's replacement. 'They calls me Crow's-Nest Jake. Ye may call me Mr Jake, if you've a mind to.'

The boys murmured as he wandered over to the same window that Miss Bronteen was wont to haunt and turned his back to them, just as she had done on so many occasions.

'Arrr. Before we begin the lesson,' he said, staring off towards the moors, 'I thought we might hear a bit of poetry. For sentimental reasons, I've always been partial to the Gloomy Poets myself. Now who'll start us off with a rendition of "A Song to Sorrow" by Lord D'Spond? Perhaps the barnacle-headed boy at the front?'

Everyone looked at Sponge, who rolled his eyes

and opened his book, filling his lungs and beginning with as much gusto as he could.

'O *Certain Death*, O –'

'O sir,' interrupted Newboy. 'I notice you are staring off towards the moors. Is there any special reason why, sir?'

The boys gasped and Sponge scowled. He was rather tired of being interrupted in full flow. The pirate teacher turned to face them.

'Arrr,' he said, peering at Newboy. 'As a matter of fact there is a tale, if you've the belly to hear it.'

The boys nodded. What could be worse than the Gloomy Poets?

'Arrr. It all began when I was a young sprat, not much older than you are now. Ye'll be surprised to know I hail from this here part of the map.'

The boys muttered and mumbled their surprise.

'I met a fair maiden from here-abouts and we fell in love. Met her on these very mist-muffled moors when I fell from my horse. I loved her more than my own ears. I loved her like a jellyfish loves her jelly babies.

But her father didn't think I was good enough for her. We didn't care about that – or so I thought.

'One day a messenger came to tell me she had run away to become an accountant. I was devastated. I felt like my heart had been ripped out by a rabid batfish and harpooned by a narwhal.

'I decided there and then to leave everything and everyone I knew and set out on a life at sea. I travelled to Liverpool and offered myself as crew on the first ship available. One that was sailing for the North Indies.'

Mr Jake returned to the window and stared out at the symphony of grey before him. A sigh of immeasurable sadness issued forth, like that of a disappointed yak.

'And when did you decide to become a teacher?' asked Newboy.

The boys gasped and stared at Newboy. Mr Jake turned to face them as though waking from a trance.

'A teacher?' he said. 'Arrr. But I'm not ... Oh – a teacher. Aye. It was, er, a quality of life thing. I wanted to spend more time with my, er, fish.'

'Your fish?' said Newboy.

'Aye,' said the pirate, scowling. 'Never mind all that, ye swabs. That's enough about me. What say I tell you some tales of terror – strange yarns of the sea and sea-faring folk?'

The boys shrugged and nodded.

'I have a tale for you,' he said, wild-eyed. 'It's not for the faint-hearted, mind. I wouldn't want to frighten you young pups. How say you?'

Just then, there was a knock at the door and the replacement for Miss Pernickety, Toothless Dave, entered.

'Arrr,' he growled. 'Sorry to interrupt, Jake. The Cap'n – I mean Headmaster – wants to have a word with a couple of these here codfish.'

'Arrr,' said Mr Jake. 'Which ones?'

'Two of their number by the names of Mildred and Sludge.'

Kenningworth pointed at Mildew and Sponge.

'Here they are, sir,' he said with a grin.

Captain Cutlass

Toothless Dave led the boys to the Headmaster's office, where the Pirate Head-master, parrot on shoulder, sat at the Headmaster's desk while several other members of the pirate staff stood about, looming menacingly.

'Arrr. Now, then,' said the Pirate Headmaster. 'What say we have a little chat, me hearties?'

'A chat?' said Sponge nervously. 'Yes. That sounds lovely. Doesn't it, Mildew? A chat. We like a chat, don't we? Oh yes, we –'

'I'm sorry,' said Mildew, putting his hand over Sponge's mouth. 'He babbles when he's scared.'

'Arrr. There be nothing to be scared of. Ain't that right, boys?'

'I feels I must object to the word "boys" in this context,' said Nevermiss Nellie.

'Aye!' said Mizzenmast Mary. 'She's right.'

'Same goes for "lads" and "guys", to be fair,' said Leather-Nose Susan, the replacement music teacher. 'It's patronising.'

'All right, all right,' said the Pirate Headmaster, clenching his fists. 'I respect your views and your right to express it, mateys. I just wish you'd raise these concerns through the proper channels. You can see how it be undermining my authority. We've spoken about this afore.'

He sighed. The pirate teachers mumbled and grumbled but gradually settled down under the fierce gaze of the Pirate Headmaster. He looked back towards Mildew and Sponge.

'Arrr. Where was I? Oh yes. Now a little bird tells me you two know more than most about the treasure of the *Golden Skull*,' continued the Pirate Headmaster.

Mildew and Sponge glared at the parrot and the parrot glared back.

'Arrr! Captain Cutlass here has been keeping an eye on you and reporting back,' he added.

'I *need some food, Mildew. My brain is hungry!*' said Captain Cutlass in a squeaky voice.

'That sounds nothing like me!' said Sponge.

'Actually, it's not that bad,' said Mildew.

'Come on,' said the Pirate Headmaster, pointing to Mildew. 'We know you be descended from Greenbeard. We read it in the paper. We know you've been looking for the treasure. Spill your bucket! Tell us what ye know or face the consequences!'

'Why should we?' said Mildew more boldly than he felt. 'You've already done away with the teachers. How do we know you won't do the same to us?'

The Pirate Headmaster raised his hands in a calming gesture.

'The teachers be unharmed,' he said. 'For the moment.'

Mildew and Sponge gasped.

'The spontaneous combustion thing was just a ruse,' said the Pirate Headmaster.

'Then where are they?' said Sponge.

'Arrr!' said the Pirate Headmaster. 'Now that would be telling. Get us our treasure and they'll be released and no harm done.'

'*Your* treasure?' said Mildew.

'Aye!' growled the Pirate Headmaster. 'The fact is we're all of us here descended from Greenbeard's crew.'

The others grunted their agreement.

'We be descended from those whom Greenbeard diddled out of their true rewards every time he kept those jewels for himself. That ain't the pirate way. We be here to find that treasure and take what's ours!'

A cheer went up from the crew.

'So be we,' said Mildew. 'Be'nt we, Sponge?'

'Yes,' said Sponge. 'I mean, aye.'

'Well, that's good!' said the Pirate Headmaster. 'Then you can find it for us!'

'What if we were to keep it for ourselves?'

'Ha! You think you codlings can take the treasure from us?'

The pirate crew scoffed loudly.

'How many times have I told you to close your mouths when you eat?' shouted the Pirate Headmaster. 'We're pirates, not animals!'

'Sorry, Cap'n,' mumbled the crew.

'Arrr,' said the Pirate Headmaster. 'Where was I?'

'You were casting scorn on our ability to snaffle the treasure,' said Mildew.

'Aye,' growled the Pirate Headmaster menacingly.

'You'll stow any idea of pursuing this madness, lads – if you know what's good for you, that is.'

Sponge whimpered.

'But I claim my right to the treasure under the rules of the Pirate Code,' said Mildew.

'What faldoolery is this?' said the Pirate Headmaster. 'What know ye of the Pirate Code, landlubber?'

'More than you think,' said Mildew. 'Sponge. Go to the library and fetch *Every Boy's Book of Pirates*.'

'The *Every Who's Book of What*?' cried the Pirate Headmaster.

'I'll be back in a trice,' said Sponge, heading off to the library.

Mildew waited with the pirates, an uneasy silence settling on the assembled crowd. Minutes went by. They were joined by more. Mizzenmast Mary began to whistle.

'Sorry,' said Mildew. 'His legs are quite short.'

Eventually Sponge came back, gasping, book in hand.

Mildew took it from him and flicked through the pages.

'You see!' cried Mildew. 'Rule 27, paragraph 5, sub-section 59, appendix 478c: "A descendant of a Pirate Captain, be he of sound mind, may claim the right to be governed by the rules of the Pirate Code and be given the honorary title of 'pirate'."'

The Pirate Headmaster shrugged.

'And where exactly does that get ye, shark bait?'

Mildew flicked through the pages again.

'Because,' he said, 'appendix 58a of the same rule says: "The said descendant can claim the right to the proceeds of the aforementioned ancestor, be it in gold, silver, jewels or coin of the realm, if he be responsible for their discovery."'

The Pirate Headmaster took a pair of thick-lensed glasses out of his pocket and sheepishly put them on. He saw Mildew looking at him.

'What?' he said defensively.

'I didn't say anything,' said Mildew.

'Arrr. Pirates wear glasses too, you know,' he said. 'Get over it.'

The Pirate Headmaster read the section Mildew pointed to and nodded in agreement.

'Arrr,' said the Pirate Headmaster, taking the book from Mildew and flicking through the pages. 'That would be annoying if it wasn't for the fact that in Rule 31, paragraph 7, clause 42, it says clearly: "Anyone who is captured by a pirate loses the right to any treasure they may otherwise have a justified claim to."'

There was a murmur of approval from the pirate crew. Mildew asked if he might have the book again, flicked through the pages until he found the relevant section.

'You see – Rule 261, paragraph 21, amendment 7, footnote 5c: "A pirate and his crew" – for the purposes of this I am seeing the staff and boys as my "crew" –'

'Agreed,' said the Pirate Headmaster.

'"If captured by another pirate whilst in the pursuance of treasure,"' continued Mildew, '"must be allowed the chance to discover the said treasure and will be given one day to achieve this end and none of his crew can be harmed so long as half of the treasure be handed over to their captors. But …"'

Mildew faltered and looked at Sponge.

'But?' said the Pirate Captain with a grin, taking the book from Mildew's grasp. 'Arrr. Shall I finish it for ye? "But if he fails, he and his entire crew will be made to walk the plank."'

The pirates chuckled.

'Luckily, we are not at sea, so that won't be possible,' said Mildew.

'It don't say nothing about the sea,' said the Pirate Captain. 'Arrr. I think we could always rig a plank up on one of those there towers.'

Mildew and Sponge gulped. The Pirate Headmaster conferred with the other pirates and after a few minutes turned back to the boys.

'Very well,' said the Pirate Headmaster. 'Ye have until noon tomorrow, mateys. But only till then, mark you. And no help from the others. Just you two. By rights it should just be Mildred here, but as you're only youngsters, we'll let it go.'

'But why?' said Sponge. 'We might find it quicker with the help of our crew.'

'Arrr. I don't make the rules,' said the Pirate Headmaster. 'Now, do I have your word you won't try to escape?'

'Aye,' said Mildew. 'You have my word as an honorary pirate and a Mildew.'

'Very well,' said the Pirate Headmaster. 'That's good enough for me.'

'Arrr. What are we supposed to do while we're waiting?' asked Leather-Nose Susan. 'You know how easily bored Mary gets.'

'I be needing mental stimulation,' cried Mary. 'I ain't going to apologise for an enquiring mind.'

'Well, I think you need to continue to teach the boys,' said Mildew.

'Teach?' said Jacques Blacques, cleaning his fingernails with his dagger. '*Mon Dieu!*'

'Yes,' said Mildew. 'You need to replace the teachers. It will stop the boys from becoming restless. They are already suspicious.'

'We ain't much for book-learning,' said the Pirate Headmaster. 'None of us had much by way of an education.'

'Speak for yourself!' cried Preacher Bob at the back.

'Yes,' said Charlie Two-Brushes. 'I have a masters in art history from the Sorbonne.'

The Pirate Headmaster groaned and shook his head.

'Very well, then,' he said with a sigh. 'Not all of us are what ye might call "conventionally academic". How's that?'

The pirates murmured and grumbled.

'If you'd just stop generalising,' said Mizzenmast Mary. 'That's all we ask.'

'Can we save this for the next meeting?' said the Pirate Headmaster. 'Please.'

There were a few more grumbles and mumbles but heads were nodded. The Pirate Headmaster continued:

'Arrr. Well, I suppose the squidlings talks sense. How say you all?'

There was a moment's pause while the crew looked from face to face among their comrades. Then there was a firm wave of nodding and together they said, 'Aye!'

'Incidentally,' said Mildew, 'what is your plan to find the treasure if we fail?'

'Arrr,' said the Pirate Headmaster. 'We intends to blow the place to smithereens and sort through the rubble. Saying it now, it doesn't sound very thought-through. But we just likes blowing things up.'

The pirates muttered and growled and chuckled, and Mildew and Sponge thought it was a good time to leave.

Big Brian rang the hour as they emerged into the quad and their classmates, who were eager to hear what had happened, clustered around them.

'Thank goodness you're all right!' said Newboy.

'Thanks,' said Sponge.

'What happened?'

'Mildew has saved the day,' said Sponge.

'That seems rather unlikely,' said Kenningworth. 'In what way exactly?'

Mildew and Sponge gave the assembled boys a quick recap of their meeting with the pirates. They were surprised to see that the boys were not as relieved as they'd hoped.

'You mean to tell me that if you two don't find the treasure, we will all be stepping off a plank to our doom?' said Furthermore.

'Er …' said Sponge.

'Well …' said Mildew. 'Only if we don't find it.'

'So you have an idea where it is?' said Hipflask.

'Well …' said Sponge.

'And we aren't allowed to help?' said Newboy.

Mildew and Sponge shook their heads. The boys groaned in despair.

'Anyway,' said Mildew, pulling Sponge away and scowling at this lack of confidence in their detectivating abilities. 'We need to get on.'

Sponge was whimpering when they came to a stop well out of earshot of the others.

'What have we done?' said Sponge. 'What if we fail?'

'You're not going to fail,' said a voice. Newboy, unnoticed by Mildew or Sponge, had come over to join them. 'I believe in you.'

'Thank you,' said Sponge.

'Yes – thank you, Newboy, old muffin,' said Mildew. 'Have a little faith, Sponge, because I know what the clue means! I *am high but my voice is low.* I've got it! Come, Sponge – to the Trembling Tower!'

Big Brian

Mildew and Sponge left Newboy in the quad and set off for the entrance to the tower.

'It came to me when Big Brian rang,' said Mildew.

'Really?' said Sponge. 'Why?'

'Because the clue is talking about Big Brian!'

'Big Brian?' said Sponge. 'The bell?'

'How many Big Brians do you know?' said Mildew.

'Well, there's that boy in the year below,' said Sponge. 'The one with the ears.'

'Yes, well –'

'And then there's the stationmaster at Lower Maudlin Station. You know, the one who –'

'Yes, yes, Sponge,' said Mildew. 'But shall we say

for the sake of argument that in all likeliness this is referring to the bell?'

Sponge nodded.

'Do you see?' Mildew went on. 'I *am high* – high up in the Trembling Tower – *my voice is low* – the horrible boom of Big Brian. High and low! Do you see?'

'You're right, Mildew,' said Sponge. 'Although how can the treasure be buried in a bell?'

'Maybe it's just taking us to another clue.'

Sponge groaned.

'Anyway, we won't find out by chatting about it down here. We need to get up the tower right now. The lives of our fellow pupils may depend on it!'

The boys moved as fast as their feeble legs would take them, and moments later they were standing at the foot of the stairway that hugged the walls as it rose into the gloom high above their heads. Looking up the middle, they could just make out the shape of Big Brian, visible only as a distant speck.

'We need to allow ourselves the maximum time to get up the tower before Big Brian rings. Imagine how deafening it will be up there! Wait here, Sponge. Any minute now …'

Bong! Bong! Bong! Bong! Bong! Bong! Bong! Bong! Bong! Bong! Bong!

The boys clung to the walls at the foot of the stairs while the whole building shook, showering plaster dust in all directions.

'Right,' said Mildew, his eyes still wobbling back into place. 'We have an hour to get up the tower and find the map before he bongs again! Come on! There's no time to lose.'

Mildew and Sponge set off up the stairs as fast as they could. Which was not at all fast. Or far. In fact, after two flights of stairs the boys collapsed, exhausted.

'How much further?' gasped Sponge.

Mildew staggered to his feet and, leaning over the balustrade, looked up at the bell, only faintly visible in the distance.

'Not far now, old scone,' he whimpered. 'Not far now.'

On and on they went – on and on and on – getting slower and slower with each new step, gasping and spluttering like exhausted otters.

'How long do we have now before Big Brian rings?' said Sponge.

'I don't know,' said Mildew. 'I fear it may not be –'

At that very moment Big Brian rang. Then rang again. And again and again and again and again and again and again and again and again and again and again.

It took a little while for the boys to stop shaking.

'At least now we have a whole hour to search for the treasure,' said Mildew.

'What?' said Sponge.

'What?' said Mildew.

'At least we have a whole hour to look for the treasure,' said Sponge.

'What?' said Mildew.

It took a few more minutes for either boy to hear anything except the persistent echo of Big Brian in their ears.

'In retrospect it was perhaps a mistake to investigate the tower at midday, Mildew,' said Sponge.

'Agreed,' said Mildew. 'But here we are. Let's get on with the search.

The boys set about trying to discover the whereabouts of the next clue.

'But where is the clue, Mildew?' said Sponge eventually, after several minutes of fruitless searching. 'I can't see it anywhere.'

'Wait. It must be on the bell,' said Mildew. 'Look! There. I can see something scratched into the metal.'

'But it's too small,' said Sponge. 'I can't read it.'

'Me neither,' said Mildew.

'I could go back and get the telescope my Uncle Tarquin gave me.'

'I fear a repetition of that climb would take hours and kill you before you reached this point.'

Sponge was forced to agree.

'But surely we can't have come all the way up here to fail?' said Sponge.

'Fail?' said Mildew. 'Never. One of us will have to climb on to the bell and read it up close. How is your head for heights, Sponge?'

'My head for heights?' said Sponge. 'Why are we discussing my head and not yours?'

'Because you are far more agile than I am, Sponge, clearly.'

'I can't say I've ever noticed that,' said Sponge.

'Really? It's always being remarked upon.'

'By whom?' said Sponge.

'I don't know,' said Mildew. 'Generally.'

'I'm not doing it,' said Sponge firmly.

Mildew knew when he saw the firm set of his friend's feeble jaw that there would be no changing his mind, so he edged his way to the balustrade and looked over. He saw the staircase coiling towards the ground and felt his legs wobble. The stairwell was dark and he could not see the bottom.

'I'm scared, Sponge,' said Mildew.

'You can do it,' said Sponge.

'Can I?' said Mildew. 'Why couldn't you do it, then?'

'Ah, well,' said Sponge. 'But you're a Mildew. Think of old Greenbeard. He must have been swinging through the rigging all the time. Imagine you're him.'

Mildew nodded and imagined being Greenbeard instead of the wobbly-legged schoolboy he actually was. Sponge was right – it did make him feel braver.

Instead of clambering over Big Brian, he imagined himself climbing over the rails of a captured vessel and scrabbling up the rigging of the mainmast to replace their flag with his own – the flag of the *Golden Skull*!

All these imaginings disappeared when Mildew lost his grip and only just managed to grab the bell rope, his feet scrabbling for a footing on the slippery surface of the bell.

'Aaaargh!'

'Mildew!' cried Sponge.

'I … I … I'm all right, Sponge,' said Mildew. 'I'm all right.'

But he wasn't. He had lost his footing completely and was left dangling over the yawning shaft of the bell tower, hanging on to the bell rope until he managed to haul himself, shaking, on to the top of the bell.

'Can you see it?' called Sponge.

Mildew managed to calm himself enough to focus on the inscription. He mouthed it to himself a couple of times to make sure he had read it correctly before calling out to Sponge.

'It says: I *am surrounded by water, surrounded by land.*'

'What does that mean?' said Sponge.

'How do I know?' said Mildew, wobbling nervously on top of the bell. 'I'm just telling you what it – aaaargh!'

I AM SURROUNDED BY WATER, SURROUNDED BY LAND

Again, Mildew's foot slipped and he just managed to leap to the balustrade. Sponge helped to haul him over, and as he sat gasping for breath he spotted a familiar hairstyle approaching.

'What are you doing here, Kenningworth?' said Mildew.

'Me?' he said nonchalantly. 'I was just having a stroll.'

'A stroll?' said Sponge. 'To the top of the Trembling Tower?'

'I'm trying to build up my calves,' said Kenningworth.

'Oh,' said Sponge. 'Well, that would certainly –'

'What are you doing really, Kenningworth?' said Mildew. 'You already have obscenely large calves. Did you follow us?'

'Follow you?' he said. 'Ha! I wouldn't follow you into a sweet shop! Even if I was already inside.'

Mildew and Sponge exchanged a puzzled glance. A loud squawk made all three boys jump and they turned to see Captain Cutlass perched on a nearby window sill.

'*Obscenely large calves!*' shrieked the parrot, before flying away out of the window.

'What an annoying creature,' said Kenningworth.

'Look, we don't want the pirates to think you're helping us,' said Mildew. 'Go away.'

'You go away,' said Kenningworth.

'Sponge and I were just leaving. Come, Sponge.'

The two boys found going down the long staircase a lot less of an ordeal than climbing it, but it was still exhausting and they arrived, jelly-legged, at the bottom.

'Where have you two been?' said Kenningworth, strolling towards them.

The two boys stared at Kenningworth, back up the stairs and then back to Kenningworth.

'How?' said Mildew. 'How?'

Kenningworth shook his head.

'I swear you two get dimmer and dimmer every day,' he said and wandered off.

'I don't understand,' said Sponge. 'He was behind us.'

'Perhaps we were mistaken,' said Mildew.

'About what?' said Sponge.

'I don't know, do I?' said Mildew. 'It's in the nature of being mistaken, isn't it?'

'What is?'

'Confusion.'

'What?'

'Exactly,' said Mildew.

'Perhaps there are two Kenningworths,' said Sponge.

'What an appalling idea,' said Mildew. 'There must be another explanation or else I'll never sleep again.'

'Do you think he heard the clue?' said Sponge. 'And what's he up to anyway? He knows the school and all of us are in deadly danger. What's he playing at?'

'Who knows,' said Mildew. 'But he's always up to something. All the more reason for us to work it out quickly and get to the treasure before him.'

Maudlin Mere

T he boys stood in the dormitory and repeated the clue over and over again but nothing occurred to either of them.

'I *am surrounded by water, surrounded by land*,' said Sponge for the umpteenth time.

'How can something be surrounded by water and land at the same time?' said Mildew.

Sponge shook his head.

'Surrounded by water,' said Sponge. 'What could that be?'

'A fish?' suggested Mildew. 'A duck? A ship? The *Golden Skull* maybe?'

'Or an island,' said Sponge.

'Yes!' said Mildew. 'But surrounded by land? That could be anything. We're surrounded by land, Sponge – shovelfuls.'

'But it says surrounded by water *and* by land.'

'But how could something be surrounded by water and land?' said Mildew.

'A lake! What about the island on Maudlin Mere, Mildew?' said Sponge. 'That's surrounded by both!'

Sponge went to the window and Mildew joined him. There, just visible in the persistent drizzle, was Maudlin Mere and the island with its single tree in the centre.

'Perhaps the treasure is buried there,' said Sponge. 'Maybe old Greenbeard buried it on an island after all!'

'I think you're right, Sponge. Well done! Come on!'

They hadn't gone more than a few paces when Newboy stepped out in front of them.

'How's it going?' he asked.

'We've solved the next clue,' said Sponge.

'Good,' said Newboy. 'The chaps are very worried. I'm afraid Kenningworth is sowing discontent.'

'I bet he is,' said Sponge.

'I've told them you're doing your best.'

'Thanks, Newboy,' said Mildew. 'Sorry – we have to dash.'

'Of course. Good luck!'

The boys waved farewell to Newboy and hurried out of the school and down the drive, through the main gate and out of the school grounds. Neither had ever been this far from the school unaccompanied. Soon they were out on the open road with no other company than the mew of a distant buzzard.

'What are we going to do when we get to Maudlin Mere?' said Sponge.

'We'll get the boat from the boathouse and row out to the island,' said Mildew.

Sponge began to turn a pale shade of a green shade of grey.

'I'm not very good on boats,' he said.

Mildew sighed.

'Come on, Sponge! It's no good telling me to imagine being Greenbeard if my first mate is going to get seasick in a boat on a lake.'

'First mate?' said Sponge. 'Really?'

'Arrr!' said Mildew. 'Of course! Who else would be my first mate?'

Sponge brightened immediately, imagining himself standing next to Mildew Greenbeard on the deck of the *Golden Skull* as they spied an island on the horizon and set sail.

'Arrr!' cried Sponge. 'Let's get the boat from the boathouse!'

'Aye-aye, matey,' said Mildew.

The boys hurried to the boathouse and climbed

into one of the rowing boats, wobbling furiously and almost capsizing before they managed to sit down and push themselves off. Sponge's new-found piratical pluck failed him.

'Arrr. I don't like the sea,' whimpered Sponge. 'It be giving me the wibbles.'

'Oh, everything be giving you the wibbles,' said Mildew. 'You'll be fine. And it's hardly the sea anyway, is it?'

'Maybe not,' said Sponge. 'But it be a very large lake. And what about the Maudlin Worm?'

'Arrr. There be no such thing as the Maudlin Worm,' said Mildew. 'There has never been the slightest proof at all.'

'That's just it,' said Sponge. 'No one ever sees the Maudlin Worm until it be too late.'

'Then how does anyone know it exists?' said Mildew.

'Because ... because ... Stop trying to confuse me, Mildew.'

'Sorry, old nut,' said Mildew. 'But you must put all wibbles about the Maudlin Worm out of your mind.'

Sponge nodded, but his eyes flickered nervously, scrutinising every ripple. The lake felt curiously remote, despite Maudlin Towers being visible in the distance.

The boys each grabbed an oar and they began to row across to the island, the irregular splash of the wooden blades seemingly the only sound for miles around.

A few minutes later the prow of the boat struck the island and the boys clambered inexpertly ashore.

'What are we looking for?' said Sponge.

'I don't know,' said Mildew.

'Look – there!'

Mildew could see it too, now. Hanging round the trunk of the tree on a rusting chain was a lead plaque. It had been there so long the tree had begun to grow around it. Were they to come back years later, they would probably find it completely enveloped and illegible. The inscription read:

'One of what ring?' said Sponge. 'Is it something to do with the jewels?'

'It beats me, Sponge,' said Mildew. 'A necklace maybe? A jewel that looks like a crow?'

'A crow?'

'Yes – rooks are those crows you see in the fields hereabouts.'

'The ones that live in rookeries.'

'The same,' said Mildew. 'That's probably where they get their name.'

'Unless … rookeries are named after rooks?'

Mildew pondered this.

'Perhaps. Anyway, never mind that. Let's get off this place and work it out back at the school.'

They got into the boat. However, while they had been on the island a thick fog had rolled across the lake and they could see nothing in any direction. They were enclosed in a void, able only to make out a few yards ahead of them.

'Mildew,' said Sponge tremulously. 'I don't like it.'

'Nor do I, Sponge,' said Mildew. 'But we must be brave. Which way is the boathouse, do you think?'

'Which way is the sun?' said Sponge.

'If we could see the sun we wouldn't need to see it, would we?' said Mildew.

'I suppose ...' said Sponge.

'Come on,' said Mildew. 'It's this way, I'm sure. I can sense it. Perhaps I have inherited Greenbeard the Pirate's navigational skills.'

After twenty-five minutes they crashed into the island again, the impact almost throwing them both out of the boat and into the murky waters of the mere.

'Curses!' hissed Mildew. 'Arrr. I told you your oar was at the wrong angle.'

'The wrong angle?' said Sponge. 'How are you an expert on oar angles all of a sudden?'

The fog was still impenetrable, but neither had an appetite for spending any more time on the island. They pushed off again. They had not been going for many minutes when a shape started to become visible in the nebulous mist ahead.

'Aaaargh!' cried Sponge. 'The Maudlin Worm!'

'In a way you're right,' said Mildew as the shape now became more distinct.

'Kenningworth!' said Sponge.

The other boat drew alongside.

'What be you doing here?' said Mildew.

'Oh, stop talking like a pirate, you nostril. I've got as much right to go boating on the mere as you two,' said Kenningworth.

'In the fog?' said Mildew.

'I like the fog,' said Kenningworth. 'It's good for my complexion.'

'I bet it is,' said Mildew.

'It is, I just told you,' said Kenningworth.

'Maybe you did, maybe you didn't,' said Mildew.

'I did,' said Kenningworth. 'Tell him, Sponge.'

Sponge opened his mouth to speak but Mildew cut him off.

'Never mind, never mind,' he said. 'Look, what are you up to, Kenningworth?'

'We'll see, won't we?'

'Maybe we will,' said Mildew.

'I just said we will.'

'Well, then,' said Mildew. 'I suppose we …'

But Kenningworth had already disappeared into the mists. Mildew and Sponge picked up their oars and began to row, delighted to strike the jetty that was just a few yards from the boathouse. They climbed out and headed back to the school.

Resembling a Rook

Mildew and Sponge scuttled up the drive towards the school gates, looking back over their shoulders every now and then for any sign of Kenningworth. They were also both trying to make sense of the clue from the island on Maudlin Mere.

'I *am one of a ring and resemble a rook*,' said Sponge. 'I *am one of a ring and resemble a rook. I am one of a ring and resemble a rook. I am one of a ring and resem–*'

'You can stop doing that whenever you like, Sponge,' said Mildew. 'As long as it's right now.'

'I thought it might help.'

'Then you were mistaken.'

'Aaargh!' said Sponge as he saw a group of the pirate teachers standing in the path right ahead of them, cutlasses and pistols drawn.

'Arrr!' said the Pirate Headmaster. 'Where's my treasure?'

'*Our* treasure, I think ye mean,' said Mizzenmast Mary.

'Aye, aye,' said the Pirate Headmaster. 'Of course. Our treasure.'

The pirates leaned towards the boys and growled.

'Now see here,' said Mildew, 'we still have hours yet.'

'We be impatient though,' said the Pirate Headmaster. 'Especially Toothless Dave.'

'Yes,' said Toothless Dave. 'Hurry up and find Greenbeard's Ghost.'

The pirate teachers gasped and looked around, wide-eyed and terror-struck.

'Sorry – I meant treasure,' said Toothless Dave.

The pirate teachers sighed and relaxed.

'You're scared,' said Mildew.

'Arrr!' said the Pirate Headmaster. 'No, we ain't!'

'Yes, you are,' said Mildew. 'That's why you're happy for us to find the treasure for you. You're scared you might meet Greenbeard's Ghost!'

'Stop saying his name!!' yelled the Pirate Headmaster. 'No sense in calling for him, is there?'

'For who? *Greenbeard's Ghost?*' said Mildew.

'Arrr!' growled the Pirate Captain, clamping his hands over his ears. 'Perhaps it'd be better if we left you boys to it.'

'Aye!' agreed the crew, who were all nervously looking this way and that.

The pirates left in a hurry and the boys returned to their clue-cracking, the crunch of gravel underfoot the only sound in the landscape.

'What could you have a ring of?' said Mildew after a while. 'And how could it look like a rook?'

'Biscuits,' said Sponge without hesitation.

'Why biscuits?' said Mildew.

'It was the first thing that came into my head.'

'I worry about you sometimes, Sponge,' said Mildew. 'Shall we try again? What things – that aren't biscuits – could be described as being in a ring?'

Sponge's face twisted into concentration.

'Cats?' suggested Sponge.

Mildew stared at him.

'I really don't know, Mildew,' said Sponge eventually.

They were just about to re-enter the school gates when Mildew skidded to a halt.

'Wait!' said Mildew. 'What's that circle of stones we pass on the way to Maudlin Towers from Lower Maudlin? Is a circle not also a ring?'

'The Stones of Maudlin!' cried Sponge. 'Yes! That is a ring. A ring of stones. You've cracked it, Mildew! We just have to find one that looks like a rook.'

Instead of returning to school, the two boys hurried back in the direction of the mere and Maudlin Marshes.

The ancient circle of lichen-and-weed-covered stones had stood on a piece of high ground at the edge of the marshes since time immemorial. The two boys approached the marshes with great trepidation. Every boy at Maudlin Towers had been told to avoid them. Many had disappeared without trace over the years and they were keen not to add to the number.

Grabbing long sticks, they poked their way forward, jumping from relatively dry hummock to relatively dry hummock, squelching as they went, trying to avoid the oozing, slimy mud and sodden peat bog that seemed intent on devouring them.

As they finally reached more solid ground and approached the Stones of Maudlin, the clouds parted and a shaft of sunlight beamed down as though the stones were actors on a stage.

'Strange to think that Miss Livia might have seen these same stones,' said Mildew, overawed momentarily by the majesty of the sight.

'I suppose she might have seen them from the attic window,' said Sponge. 'On a clear day. If her eyesight was unimpaired.'

Mildew sighed.

'In Roman times, Sponge,' he said. 'I was making a lyrical observation about the great antiquity of these pebbles. They were already ancient when the Romans moved in. It's amazing when you think about it. Imagine all those hairy druids cavorting about.'

'They say the stones were once giants,' said Sponge, 'turned to boulders by a mighty druid.'

'*They*?' Sponge.

'People,' said Sponge. 'You know ...'

'Never listen to people, Sponge. They talk the most idiotic piffle.'

'Possibly,' said Sponge. 'But it's easy to believe they are the products of magic, Mildew. Look at them.'

Mildew shrugged, looking at the stones.

'They don't seem especially large for giants,' said Mildew, rolling his eyes.

'People were smaller back then,' said Sponge.

'They were certainly more gullible,' said Mildew.

Sponge scowled. The light changed again and the stones were cast into deep shadow, all colour stolen from the scene, leaving only shades of gloom.

'They also say that no one can count the stones,' said Sponge mysteriously. 'Because they keep moving.'

'Is this "people" again?' said Mildew.

Sponge nodded sheepishly.

'I think that says more about the consistently low maths ability in the Maudlin area than it does about the supposed magical properties of the stones. In any case, which is it? Are they stone giants or can they move about?'

'You have no feel for the supernatural, Mildew,' said Sponge, frowning. 'That's the whole point of the supernatural. It can be whatever it wants. The Partworks are a very spiritual sort.'

'Are they?' said Mildew. 'What about the Spongelys?'

'The Spongelys have no defining features.'

The boys walked around the circle looking for a rook-like stone. They examined it from seemingly every angle, but none of them looked remotely like a crow of any kind.

'What about that one?' said Sponge.

'That looks more like a rabbit than a rook, Sponge.'

The boys sighed. It seemed hopeless. Were they really going to fall at this hurdle?

'It's been so long since Greenbeard was here,' said Mildew, 'perhaps the stone has lost its beak or its wing or whatever.'

Sponge nodded. It was certainly possible. These stones had been battered by all the weather Cumberland could throw at them. Who knew what shape they used to be all those years ago.

'We can only hope the inscription is still there,' said Mildew. 'We'll just have to check them all.'

'Wait!' said Sponge. 'Look – that one.'

'That doesn't look anything like a rook, Sponge. It's almost got battlements along the top like a castle.'

'Exactly!' said Sponge. 'Not a rook as in a crow, but a rook as in a chess piece – the castle!'

'By Jupiter, I think you're right, Sponge!'

They went to the stone and began to search the surface for any sign of an inscription. Sponge pulled back a piece of bracken and there it was.

'Look here – there's something scratched into the surface. Can you read it?'

'I think so,' said Mildew, peering at the scratched-out lettering . . .

They looked at the inscription. They looked at the stone, at its neighbours, then at each other. The stones were almost identical in size. The boys looked back at the inscription. They looked back at each other. They shrugged.

'Wait,' said Sponge. 'I thought I saw something moving.'

'Oh, Sponge,' said Mildew. 'You are so suggestible. The Stones of Maudlin don't really move. It's a legend. Like Australia.'

'But I swear, Mildew – look!'

Mildew sighed and turned slowly round, following with withering reluctance his friend's trembling and pointing finger.

'See? The one with the tangle of ferns growing out of it.'

Mildew's eyes widened as one of the stones seemed to edge slowly behind one of the others in the circle.

'So the legend is true!' cried Sponge.

'Wait a moment,' said Mildew. 'I recognise that tangle of ferns. Kenningworth – come out!'

After a few seconds, the suspected moving Stone of Maudlin did indeed reveal itself to be none other than Kenningworth.

'What are you doing following us again?' said Sponge.

'Following you?' said Kenningworth. 'I often come down to the Stones to be alone with my thoughts.'

'Alone with your thoughts?' said Mildew. 'I doubt very much that you have more than one at a time.'

'It varies,' said Kenningworth. 'I have all kinds of thoughts.'

'I bet you do,' said Sponge.

'Well, you'd win that bet, because I do. As I said.'

'What?' said Sponge.

'Exactly,' said Kenningworth.

Sponge blinked, as he often did when bedazzled or bebaffled.

'Don't bandy words with him, Sponge,' said Mildew. 'We have urgent business elsewhere.'

'Where?' said Kenningworth.

'Wouldn't you like to know,' said Sponge.

'Yes – I would,' said Kenningworth. 'Else I would hardly have asked, would I?'

'Well, then …' said Sponge, beginning to blink again.

'Well, then, what?' said Kenningworth.

Sponge looked to Mildew for assistance.

'None of your business, Kenningworth,' said Mildew. 'Come on, Sponge. Let's get going.'

'And don't follow us,' said Sponge, turning round.

But Kenningworth had disappeared. The Stones of Maudlin stood deserted and inscrutable once more.

'Where did he go?' said Sponge.

'Never mind him,' said Mildew. 'Come on. And I've realised what the clue means. The bothy!'

'I *am small but my neighbour is lofty* … Of course! It stands in the shadow of lofty old Maudlin Towers. How strange that everything should come back to the place where our previous adventures began.'

'Yes,' said Mildew. 'But hurry – it's getting dark. There's no time to lose.'

The boys were just about to head off to the bothy when they saw Captain Cutlass sitting on one of the fallen Stones of Maudlin.

It fixed them with its one good eye and squawked.

'*The bothy!*'

'Is that really supposed to be me?' said Mildew as the parrot flapped away towards Maudlin Towers.

'I hate that bird,' said Sponge.

Back to the Bothy

Mildew and Sponge cut through the school on their way to the sports field and the bothy and the boys were waiting for them.

'Have you found the treasure, Mildew?' said Enderpenny.

'Why are you only asking Mildew?' said Sponge.

'Well, have you?' said Furthermore as everyone looked at Sponge.

'No,' admitted Sponge. 'Not yet.'

'But we're close!' said Mildew.

'Are we?' said Sponge.

'Of course we –'

'The pirates have already fixed the plank up on the Tottering Tower,' Filbert interrupted him.

'You need to find that treasure, Mildew!' said Kenningworth.

'Well, we'd do it a lot quicker if you didn't keep getting in the way.'

'What are you talking about?' said Kenningworth. 'I haven't been anywhere near you. You're raving.'

'Come on, Sponge,' said Mildew. 'We haven't got time for banter. We've got a school to save. Have no fear, boys. We won't let you down.'

Mildew paused for the cheer he had hoped would follow this declaration, but when all that came was a communal groan, he nodded to Sponge and they headed off towards the sports field.

'Psst,' came a voice behind them.

'Newboy,' said Sponge, turning round.

'I was right about Kenningworth,' said Newboy. 'He's still planning to thwart you and grab the treasure for himself.'

'I have to say, I know it's Kenningworth but I'm amazed that even he would let his fellows plummet to their doom,' said Mildew.

'He's deranged,' said Newboy. 'I think he's capable of anything.'

The boys nodded solemnly, and after taking their leave of Newboy once more, Mildew and Sponge scuttled through the school towards the field and the bothy, as they had done so many times on their last adventure, memories flooding back with every step. It was properly dark now. A full moon had risen but was obscured by cloud. It was getting difficult to see where they were going.

'It feels a bit odd being given permission to roam wherever we like, Mildew,' said Sponge as they edged along.

'Yes, I know what you mean. But I suppose the regime of pirates was always going to be a bit more lax.'

'Where do you think the teachers are, Mildew? Assuming they are still alive.'

'I don't know, Sponge,' said Mildew. 'We haven't got time to find them *and* the treasure. One thing at a time.'

'It's a bit creepy,' said Sponge, 'wandering round the grounds at night.'

'Surely we should be ready for anything after our last adventure,' said Mildew with a smile. 'You faced down a werewolf, after all.'

'I know,' said Sponge. 'The trouble is, that has made me even more nervous about what might be out there.'

'Out where?'

'Everywhere,' said Sponge, nervously looking around. 'In the dark. I know I won't see a werewolf again, thank goodness, but there are plenty of other things that might be lurking.'

'Like what?' said Mildew, a little nervous himself now.

'A ghost for one thing.'

Mildew rolled his eyes.

'What if the ghost of Greenbeard is waiting for us?' said Sponge.

'You heard Mr Luckless,' said Mildew. 'That's just a story to give simple folk the frights. You saw what those pirates were like when we mentioned the ghostly Greenbeard.'

'But I don't like ghosts either, Mildew,' said Sponge.

'Sponge. You are obsessed. We are not going to see a ghost. Fear not.'

Just then, a figure loomed out of the darkness towards them. A tall figure wearing a suit and teacher's gown. A man with a familiar shock of white hair.

'Mr Particle!' said Mildew and Sponge as one.

'Boys,' said their departed physics teacher, clearly as surprised to see them as they were to see him. 'Is everything all right? You look like you've seen a ghost.'

'But …' began Sponge, his whole body quivering like a jelly on a bicycle.

'Ah – boys,' said Mr Particle a little shiftily. 'What on earth are you doing here anyway?'

'What are *we* doing here?' said Mildew, staring.

'Yes,' said Mr Particle. 'Why are you roaming the school grounds after lights out?'

'We … that is … er, Sponge, tell Mr Particle.'

'What? Erm … well …'

'I think it's best you return to the dorm, boys,' said Mr Particle. 'And don't you owe me some home-work, Mildew?'

At that moment the beaky nose of a gargoyle broke free from its owner and plummeted earth-ward, striking Mr Particle on the head. He collapsed like a sack of blancmange.

'Is he d-d-d–'

'No, Sponge – merely unconscious.'

Mr Particle moaned in his sleep.

'You wouldn't have thought a ghost could be knocked unconscious, would you?' said Sponge.

Mildew had a sudden flash of inspiration and looked off towards the bothy.

'That's because he's not a ghost, Sponge,' said Mildew, prodding the physics teacher in the ear. 'Look. He's as solid as one of Mrs Glump's trifles.'

'But how? He's dead, Mildew. Completely dead. I saw him shot. He's got a grave and everything. Two if you count the first time he was buried.'

'Dead now,' said Mildew. 'But not in the past.'

Sponge frowned in concentration.

'And yet it's now now …' continued Mildew.

'Now now?' said Sponge.

'Yes – and he's alive. Now. Even though he died – back then.'

Sponge nodded hesitantly.

'And that can only mean …'

'The time machine!' they said at the same time.

'In the past, when he was still alive, he must have gone into the future – his future – which is now our present,' said Mildew. 'Do you see?'

'He's going to get a nasty shock when he finds out he's dead,' said Sponge. 'I'd hate that. And what if someone finds him? Or the time machine?'

'Yes – I can't think it would be a good idea for a time machine to get into the hands of pirates, Sponge.

Imagine them yo-ho-hoing their way through history, back and forth, back and forth. Or Kenningworth for that matter. We should get Particle back to the bothy and explain things to him when he wakes up.'

'Good idea,' said Sponge. 'Look – there. Mr Scurry's wheelbarrow. We can use that.'

The boys dragged Mr Particle's body into the wheelbarrow and with some difficulty managed to shove it along the ha-ha to the bothy.

'Right,' said Mildew. 'Let's find this next clue to the treasure.'

Mildew was just opening the door when Sponge remembered something.

'The money!' cried Sponge. 'We don't need the treasure. The Headmaster's money is in the chair!'

'Of course!' replied Mildew. 'Although I'm not sure the pirates will accept cash. They seem very settled on having Greenbeard's jewels. But that doesn't mean we can't have the money as well. The pirates need never know. If we play this right, we can return the money to the Headmaster – wherever he is – and Maudlin Towers will be saved and we will have half of Greenbeard's treasure!'

'Perhaps we should remove the money before Mr Particle wakes,' said Sponge. 'It might confuse things.'

'Agreed. You do that, Sponge, while I look for the clue.'

The two boys left Mr Particle in the wheel-barrow and went inside the bothy.

'There's a lamp over there,' said Mildew, 'with some matches beside it. Light it so we can see what we're doing.'

Sponge struck the damp match a number of times before it ignited and he lit the wick of the lamp and replaced its grimy glass cover. The interior of the bothy was flooded with amber light.

The two boys set about their search, Mildew hunting for the next clue to the treasure, while Sponge dug about into the springs and cushions of the seat, almost disappearing into its upholstery.

'Here, Sponge,' cried Mildew. 'Look. I've found it. It's an inscription above the door. It says –'

'Wait. I've found something!' cried Sponge, spotting a parcel rammed down the back of the chair. He pulled at the brown paper and it tore, revealing wads of bank notes.

'It's the money!' shouted Sponge.

'Excellent!' cried Mildew, coming to look and climbing on to the armrest to peer over Sponge's shoulder.

'It's a bit tricky to get out though. I may need your –'

As Sponge struggled to extricate himself from the chair, his backside pushed the lever. There was a familiar flash and whine.

'What have you done?' said Mildew.

'Whatever it was, I didn't mean to,' said Sponge.

'Well, did you send us to the past or the future?' said Mildew, looking about for any signs of change but seeing none.

'I have no idea,' said Sponge.

'We should just go straight back to where we were. We don't want any of that confusion. I don't think my brain could take it. We should just get the money back to the Headmaster. We'll be heroes!'

'Yes. Of course. I know what you mean,' said

Sponge. 'Although I am a little bit intrigued to see where we are. Aren't you?'

Mildew peered at the dials.

'Actually, we only appear to have journeyed a small way into the future. A matter of weeks, I'd guess.'

'It would be nice to know if we managed to save the school,' said Sponge. 'You know – to see if everything was back to normal. Normal for Maudlin, that is.'

Mildew paused as his hand moved towards the clock and lever.

'Just a peek and then straight back,' he said.

Sponge smiled and nodded. The boys jumped down from the chair and pulled open the door.

To their amazement and horror, just outside the door in front of them was a giant floating eyeball.

A Giant Floating Eyeball

'Aaaargh!!!!!' they cried, slamming the door.

'What was that?' said Sponge.

'I don't know,' said Mildew. 'But it didn't look friendly.'

'What are we going to do?' said Sponge.

'Back to the time machine!' shouted Mildew.

The boys leaped on to the chair and Mildew deftly returned the controls to neutral so they would return to the exact moment they set off and then pulled the lever.

'Where on earth did that thing come from?' said Sponge, staring at the door, shaking.

'Who knows, Sponge,' said Mildew. 'But at least it's not there now.'

'Are you sure?' said Sponge.

'Of course I'm sure,' said Mildew. 'It's in the future. Although not as far in the future as I'd like. In only a matter of weeks or even days that thing will be wandering around Maudlin Towers.'

Sponge whimpered.

'Open the door, Mildew,' he said. 'Just to make sure.'

'Why don't you open the door?' said Mildew.

'Because you are braver,' said Sponge. 'And bigger. Whatever it was will be more likely to be intimidated by you.'

'It was a giant eyeball, Sponge,' said Mildew. 'It didn't seem the sort of thing to be intimidated by a Mildew – even a Berkshire Mildew.'

'All the same ... please ...'

Mildew sighed and got down from the chair, shaking his head and rolling his eyes. With a great flourish, he threw open the door, stepping to one side to let Sponge see.

Mildew was rather surprised to note his friend's expression had returned to one of absolute horror. Mildew frowned and looked round the door himself, his own expression mirroring Sponge's as he saw standing on the threshold an enormous slavering werewolf, its fur glistening in the light from the full moon above.

'Aaaargh!' cried Mildew, slamming the door shut again. 'Old Particle is having one of his turns, Sponge.'

However, no sooner was the door shut than it flew open again, knocking Mildew flying across the bothy to land in a crumpled heap. Half dazed, he watched as the werewolf entered and closed in on the hapless Sponge, who cowered in the chair.

Mildew looked about him and saw a shovel leaning against the wall. He climbed to his feet and picked it up, walking stealthily towards the growling werewolf. He coughed.

'Excuse me. Mr Particle, sir ...'

The werewolf turned and Mildew hit it round the side of the head as hard as he could. The werewolf spun around a couple of times and Sponge just managed to leap out of the way as it slumped, unconscious into the time machine.

'Mildew!' shouted Sponge. 'You saved my life.'

'Not if he wakes up,' said Mildew. 'Quick! We need to send him off.'

'Which way?' said Sponge.

'The past of course,' said Mildew. 'We don't want to send him into the future to wait for us, do we?'

'True,' said Sponge. 'You're so –'

The were-wolf stirred.

'Aaaargh!!!'

Mildew turned the dial and yanked the lever and the time machine disappeared in a flash and a whine.

'Phew!' said Sponge.

They took a moment to catch their breath and collect their thoughts.

'Right,' said Mildew. 'Let's put that money somewhere safe until we find the Headmaster.'

'The money?' said Sponge.

'Yes, Sponge,' said Mildew. 'The money you found in the chair. The Headmaster's money. Where is it?'

Sponge looked at where the chair had been and bit his lip.

'It's still in the chair, isn't it?' said Mildew.

Sponge nodded. Mildew sighed.

'I suppose we are back to searching for the treasure,' said Sponge.

'I suppose we are,' said Mildew.

'Do you think the pirates will really keep their word?' said Sponge. 'Will they release the staff, leave the boys unharmed and hand over half the treasure?'

'I don't know, Sponge,' said Mildew. 'But what choice do we have?'

Sponge nodded.

'So what does it say?' asked Sponge. 'The clue you found?'

Mildew picked up the lamp and both boys peered up at the inscription carved into the wood over the door. It said:

I AM AT SEA AMONG THE DEAD

'What?' said Sponge. 'But surely that's the same as on the headstone in the Old Graveyard, where we started this whole thing?'

'It does appear to be,' said Mildew. 'But how? And, in a very real sense, why?'

'I suppose we'd better go and find out,' said Sponge.

Mildew nodded and replaced the lamp, blowing it out and hurling them into darkness, apart from the moonlight seeping in through the cobweb-muffled windows.

'Mildew,' said Sponge quietly. 'What was that enormous eye?'

'I don't know, old cheese. But I have a horrible feeling we will find out later in the series.'

'The series?' said Sponge.

'Yes – we've had an adventure with the time machine and Vikings and so on and now we are having another with pirates – with the occasional werewolf thrown in for good measure. I'm assuming we'll have more, so I'm calling them a series of adventures.'

'I see,' said Sponge. 'Interesting.'

Mildew opened the door and there stood a figure backlit by the moon.

'Aaargh!!!' cried the boys.

'Well, well,' said Kenningworth. 'What are you two up to?'

'You again! What are you up to more like?' said Mildew.

Kenningworth smiled but did not reply.

'How long have you been skulking about?' said Sponge.

'Long enough,' said Kenningworth.

'Long enough for what?' said Mildew.

'Wouldn't you like to know,' said Kenningworth.

'Maybe we would, maybe we wouldn't,' said Mildew.

The three boys peered at each other for a goodly amount of time.

'What was that flash and whine?' said Kenningworth eventually.

'It was Sponge,' said Mildew.

'What?' said Sponge.

'It's a medical condition,' said Mildew. 'He doesn't like to talk about it.'

Kenningworth peered at Sponge. Sponge blushed and turned away.

'Anyway,' said Mildew. 'We can't stand around blathering with the likes of you, Kenningworth. I'm ready for my bed. How about you, Sponge?'

'Yes. I am rather tuckered out, actually, now you come to mention it.'

'Feel free to linger if you want,' said Mildew to Kenningworth.

'Maybe I will,' he said.

'Then you should,' said Mildew.

'I will,' said Kenningworth.

'Good,' said Mildew.

'Oh, I know it's good,' said Kenningworth.

'You do, do you?' said Mildew.

'Yes,' said Kenningworth. 'But do you?'

'Do I what?' asked Mildew.

'Exactly,' said Kenningworth.

He shook his head while Kenningworth raised a haughty eyebrow.

'Come on, Sponge,' said Mildew. 'Enough of this piffle.'

The boys walked back to the school, their heads swimming with images of werewolves and giant floating eyeballs and extinct physics teachers, and were a little surprised to find Newboy palely loitering in the vestibule.

'What are you doing here, Newboy?' said Mildew.

'I was following Kenningworth,' he replied. 'I lost him at the ha-ha.'

'The ha-ha?' said Sponge.

'Oh, don't start all that again,' said Mildew. 'Thanks, Newboy, but worry not – we think we may be at the end of our quest. See you back at the dorm!'

'Excellent,' said Newboy.

Mildew and Sponge headed off towards the

Old Graveyard. The moon was high and full and illuminated the way as the two boys picked their way through the headstones until they found the one where their search had begun.

The two boys stared, baffled and confused. They had come full circle and were no nearer to finding the treasure, it seemed.

As they stood there, a moth fluttered in front of Sponge's face and he flapped his hands trying to shoo it away.

But the moth attracted a bat, making him shriek, and leap with exactly the agility Mildew had attributed to him, ending up on the other side of the headstone.

The moonlight was especially bright across its relatively uncluttered surface. A few tendrils of ivy were growing up the stonework but Sponge could see something inscribed between the leaves. He pulled the ivy away and was amazed at what was revealed.

'Mildew, there's a map,' cried Sponge.

'What?' said Mildew.

Mildew went round to join his friend on the other side of the headstone. Sure enough, there was a small map of the grounds just outside the west side of Maudlin Towers, with measurements and a very clear 'X' marked.

'Do you mean this was here all the time?' said Mildew. 'The clues were all a waste of time?'

'It does seem that way,' said Sponge, clearing some weeds away from the bottom of the front of the headstone. 'You see? It even says: *Or, if time is short, see reverse.*'

Mildew growled.

'Greenbeard was a bit infuriating, wasn't he?' said Mildew.

'I didn't like to say,' said Sponge. 'Him being a relative and everything. But yes. A bit.'

Mildew sighed.

The boys memorised the map and set off to the space marked 'X', pacing all the measurements out.

After a few minutes they stared down at the spot they had arrived at.

'But how?' said Sponge, frowning.

'I don't know,' said Mildew in bafflement.

But sure enough, the spot they had carefully paced out was exactly the same place Flintlock had first buried Mr Particle before digging him up again and re-burying him in the staff graveyard.

'Surely Flintlock would have found the treasure,' said Sponge. 'He dug here twice. He doesn't look like a man who has found treasure though. He eats flies. I've seen him.'

'Agreed,' said Mildew with a sigh. 'And yet this is where Greenbeard said it was buried. Maybe it was found years ago. Maybe it's all a horrible joke.'

The two boys stared at the patch of earth but there seemed nothing more to say. They both felt suddenly very tired at the day's exertions.

'What are we going to do, Mildew?' said Sponge. 'Everyone is depending on us.'

'I know,' said Mildew. 'We will have to fall on the mercy of the pirates.'

'Aren't pirates traditionally a bit merciless?' asked Sponge.

'Let's sleep on it, Sponge,' said Mildew. 'We've kept our side of the bargain. We have solved the riddles and found the site of the buried treasure.

We just need to try to work out a way of keeping that knowledge from the Pirate Headmaster while we think of a new plan.'

There was a muffled squawk above their heads and they turned to see Captain Cutlass flying away, a luminous flash of green in the night.

'Bother,' said Mildew.

A Hatch under the Rug

Mildew and Sponge's dreams were filled with ghostly physics teachers, werewolves, giant floating eyeballs and multiple Kenningworths.

Such was his exhaustion, Mildew had worried that he might sleep in, but his concerns were misplaced as the rest of the boys helpfully shook him awake as dawn broke and loomed over him threateningly.

'You haven't got time to sleep,' said Enderpenny.

'We were just getting up,' said Mildew. 'Weren't we, Sponge? ... Sponge? Sponge?'

Sponge snored on until Furthermore flicked his ear.

'Ow! What?' cried Sponge, looking about him dozily.

'He'd probably be more likely to find the treasure when he's asleep,' said Kenningworth.

'Why do you keep following us around then?' said Mildew.

'Not this again,' said Kenningworth. 'Why on earth would I follow you around?'

'Because you're trying to find the treasure for yourself!' shouted Sponge.

'What?' said Kenningworth.

'Tell them, Newboy,' said Mildew. 'Wait – where is Newboy?'

The boys looked round the room but there was no sign of Newboy.

'I haven't seen him since he sneaked out early this morning,' said Kenningworth.

'Well, you'd know all about sneaking,' said Mildew.

'Then take my word for it – he was sneaking,' said Kenningworth.

'Who cares about Newboy. Have you found the location of the treasure yet?' said Furthermore.

'In a manner of speaking, yes,' said Mildew.

'In a manner of speaking?' said Furthermore. 'What's that supposed to mean?'

'Haven't got time to explain,' said Mildew. 'Come along, Sponge.'

Ignoring the protestations of the boys, Mildew and Sponge got dressed and hurried off to the Pirate Headmaster's office. But they had hardly gone more than a few paces down the corridor before they saw Kenningworth coming towards them.

'Morning, dimwits,' he said.

Mildew and Sponge were too amazed to reply and Kenningworth continued on his way, disappearing round the corner out of sight.

'But how …?' said Mildew. 'Perhaps Newboy has an explanation – if we can find him.'

Sponge peered in the direction Kenningworth had vanished.

'Come with me,' said Sponge. 'I need to check something.'

'But, Sponge,' protested Mildew.

Sponge was resolute, however, and directed Mildew to the library, where Miss Musketoon, the pirate librarian, was still asleep in her hammock above the desk.

'I was right,' said Sponge, opening the book on hypnotism, studying it and then handing it to Mildew.

'Not this again, Sponge,' he said. 'What does it matter?'

'Maybe nothing,' said Sponge. 'But look again at the list of borrowers.'

Mildew yawned.

'Kenningworth, yes,' he said. 'We know that. I accept he hypnotised me, old –'

'Look at the most recent borrower,' Sponge interrupted him. 'We didn't see it because it's on the back of the sheet.'

Mildew's eyes boggled.

'Newboy!'

'Maybe Newboy hypnotised Kenningworth as well. No – wait – that still doesn't explain why there seem to be two of him …'

'You don't think …?' began Mildew.

'I don't think what?' said Sponge.

'That Kenningworth has somehow got his hands on the time machine? Hence the duplication.'

'No!' cried Sponge.

It was too awful to imagine.

'We can only hope that there's another explanation,' said Mildew. 'But none of this matters. We have failed to find the treasure and the pirates are free to do whatever they want with us and the school. Come on, Sponge – time to face the music.'

The boys headed towards the Pirate Headmaster's office once more.

'What's that noise?' asked Sponge as they passed the hall.

'What noise?' said Mildew.

'That noise! The thumping I told you about before.'

Sure enough, there was a faint thumping noise coming from the hall. They opened the door and stepped inside. The thumping continued. It seemed to be coming from under the floor. The boys looked at each other.

'Let's get the rug up, Sponge, and see what's there.'

They started to roll back the rug.

'Look!' said Sponge.

There was a large wooden hatch built into the floor – a hatch with a large, looped metal handle.

'Come on, Sponge,' said Mildew. 'Help me to pull it open.'

'But who knows what might be in there,' said Sponge.

'Like what?'

'I don't know,' said Sponge. 'That might be where the huge floating eyeball lives.'

'The huge floating eyeball lives in the future, Sponge,' said Mildew.

'But we are in the future,' said Sponge. 'From when we last saw it.'

'Not far enough, I don't think,' said Mildew. 'And, anyway, I doubt it could thump. What would it thump with?'

'It could just bang itself against the wood.'

'I suspect that would make a softer sound altogether.'

'I suppose,' said Sponge. 'Like a balloon.'

'Er, Sponge,' said Mildew. 'Sorry to seem a bit dim but what are we doing again?'

'We are investigating this wooden hatch,' said Sponge. 'Do try and concentrate, Mildew.'

'Sorry. Why are we doing this?'

Sponge stared at him quizzically and sighed.

'Just pull, Mildew.'

The two boys heaved with all their might.

After several efforts they managed to raise the hatch and it slammed down on to the floor to reveal a gaping hole.

The boys peered in but could see nothing at first. They could, however, hear something. Without the hatch and the rug, the thumping sound was even louder. As their eyes adjusted to the gloom, the boys saw there was a set of wooden steps leading down.

'You first, Sponge,' said Mildew.

'Why me?' said Sponge.

'Because you're smaller,' said Mildew.

'What has that to do with anything?' said Sponge.

'Well,' said Mildew, 'it's just basic physics, Sponge.'

'Is it?' said Sponge.

'Almost certainly,' said Mildew.

After a moment, Sponge edged towards the first step and gingerly began to descend, Mildew one step behind him all the way. It became darker and darker as they went down and they got slower and slower as their nerve began to fail them.

They finally reached the bottom of the steps and Mildew gazed around, trying to make sense of the various shapes in the darkness. He immediately tripped over something that he realised, with a squeal of alarm, was a human leg.

'Sponge!' he yelled.

Sponge came to his aid and immediately fell over something that turned out to be an arm.

'Mildew! I've just tripped over an arm.'

'That's odd,' said Mildew. 'I've tripped over a leg. But you're yards away, Sponge. Whoever it is must be huge. Unless ...'

They now became aware of a large group of bodies sitting around, bound and gagged and in their undergarments.

'It's the teachers!' cried Mildew. 'Go and get the rest of the boys, Sponge.'

Mildew set about trying to untie the staff. The ropes binding them were huge and the knots were baffling, but luckily Miss Mizzenmast's knot-tying

demonstration proved very useful and in a few minutes the teachers were free.

'Could you not hear me banging?' asked Mr Luckless, his head a spectacle of bumps and bruises from where he had been thumping his head on a heating pipe to attract attention.

'Sponge thought you were a ghost,' said Mildew, pointing to his friend as Sponge and the rest of the boys stampeded down the steps into the cellar.

'At least I heard it,' said Sponge breathlessly. 'I sometimes wonder if you aren't a little deaf.'

'Deaf?' said Mildew. 'I have perfect hearing. I can hear a –'

'If I might interrupt,' said the Headmaster, getting to his feet. 'We thank you for your assistance but we need to regain control of the school from these barbarians.'

Mildew and Sponge were struck by how lacking in all his usual authority the Headmaster was now that he was dressed only in his underthings.

The other staff stretched and winced. Flintlock looked particularly murderous – and ridiculous – dressed in some patched long johns and a baggy undershirt. But it was Miss Bleu who spoke for them all.

'Where are zose filthy pirates?' she growled. 'What 'ave zose monsters been doing? 'Ave zey 'urt you?'

'No,' said Hipflask. 'They have actually been rather illuminating. Arrr.'

'I suppose they have been drunk and caroused about the place,' said Mr Luckless, frowning.

'No,' said Enderpenny. 'Miss Nevermiss says that be a rather offensive caricature of the pirate life and pirates can actually be very sensitive coves if you just take the time to get to know 'em.'

'What?' said the Headmaster. 'Why are you talking like that? Miss Nevermiss? Sensitive pirates?

What nonsense is this? What about the school? Have they wreaked havoc?'

'The Pirate Headmaster has installed ramps here and there,' said Furthermore. 'He be surprised by the limited access around the school. In fact, his actual words were: "Arrr, it be a shameful scandal!"'

'Oh, really?' said the Headmaster. 'Is that right?'

'To be fair, I did mention that at the last staff meeting,' said Mr Scurry, the caretaker. 'At my last school the access was much more –'

'Be that as it may,' said the Headmaster, interrupting. 'I will not have some pirate claiming to take my place. What exactly have they been doing?'

Mildew and Sponge looked at each other.

'Actually, they've been … teaching,' said Mildew.

There was a sharp intake of breath from all the staff and then a look of fury the like of which none of the boys would forget their entire lives.

'Teaching?' said the staff.

'Aye,' said the boys.

'They have crossed a line!' said the Headmaster with a steely glint in his eyes. 'To me, staff! Let's show those pirates who they are dealing with. For Maudlin Towers!'

'For Maudlin Towers!' cried the staff.

For the Love of Books

Mildew and Sponge followed the teachers out of the cellar as they thundered up the steps. The Headmaster led them to his office, but it was deserted.

Miss Pernickety said the Headmaster had a spare gown in a cupboard but he told her there was no time. However, when she opened the cupboard doors she called to him to come and see.

The cupboard was filled with the pirates' discarded clothes – and weapons. The teachers grinned and within seconds they were dressed and armed.

The boys saw no reason why they should be left out and started arming themselves to the teeth. Mildew found himself a tricorn hat, sash and cutlass, and Sponge took up a broad-brimmed

hat and a pair of pistols.

'Still no sign of Newboy?' said Mildew.

'No,' said Sponge. 'He seems to have disappeared.'

The staff emerged from the school to find the pirates outside arguing about what to do next. The teachers were on them in a flash but, just as the attack began, a long, pitch-dark carriage galloped up the drive of the school, pulled by horses, black as midnight, with long, feathered plumes on their heads.

The driver pulled the reins and the carriage screeched sideways, spraying gravel everywhere. It came to a halt, steam rising from the horses' backs. Written in gold down the side of the carriage was the word: *Governors*.

The driver, who was dressed in a black cape with a tall hat and dark glasses, banged his cane and the carriage door swung open. Out stepped twelve men and women, dressed from head to foot in black.

The tallest man strode forward, a crimson sash across his chest, a sabre swinging from his hip in a snakeskin scabbard.

'I,' he cried, 'am Sir Brashly Bugle, the Chair of Governors! What the Dickens is occurring?'

The rest of the governors grouped behind him,

Sir Brashly Bugle

gazing heroically this way and that, armed with swords and pistols and those spiky things knights sometimes have that look a bit like metal conkers.

'Back off!' cried the Headmaster with a swish of his cutlass. 'This is personal!'

The teachers attacked, each one seeking out the pirate who had taken their place in the school. Reverend Brimstone's battle with Preacher Bob was an especially violent clash, with Preacher Bob begging for mercy after only a few moments.

The boys provided moral support from a safe distance. Mildew and Sponge marvelled at the brutal efficiency with which the pirates were rounded up at sword point and herded into a muttering group in the centre of the quad, Captain Cutlass squawking in complaint.

'Arrr,' said the Pirate Headmaster to the Headmaster. 'Ye have spirit, I'll give you that. In other circumstances I'd be happy to sail with you.'

'I hardly think that likely,' said the Headmaster proudly. 'We are teachers, sir! There is no finer calling. We are not thieves. Rather we are guardians. We are keepers of the treasury that is education!'

'Miss Bronteen?' whispered Sponge.

'Sssh,' said Miss Bronteen. 'The Headmaster is speaking.'

'But it's important, miss,' said Sponge. 'The pirate called Crow's-Nest Jake is none other than your long-lost love. The one you told us about in class.'

Mildew nodded as Miss Bronteen turned to face them. Her frown became a smile as she saw that the boys were not teasing her. She peered at the group of pirates.

'Can it be true?' she said. 'All these long years, I always hoped I might see him once again, striding through the drizzle.'

The Headmaster was still delivering a speech on the wonder that is a life in teaching when he was interrupted by a cry from the heart.

'Wait!' cried Miss Bronteen.

The Headmaster, teachers, pirates, Chair of Governors, governors and schoolboys all turned to see Miss Bronteen walking towards the pirates, a previously unseen look of rapture on her face.

Jake watched Miss Bronteen approach and their eyes met, as they must have done so many times on wind-tousled Maudlin Moor in days of yore. Everything came to a hushed halt.

'My love!' cried Miss Bronteen.

'Arrr. My heart!' cried Crow's-Nest Jake. 'Is it true? Can it really be you?'

'Yes! 'Tis I!'

'Miss Bronteen!' said the Headmaster with a scowl. 'I hardly think it proper to –'

'Stow it, landlubber,' cried Miss Bronteen. 'I am bound for the seven seas. Heave ho, me hearties!'

And with this colourful outburst, she bounded into the arms of her beloved and kisses were showered in all directions.

'O my love,' said Crow's-Nest Jake. 'Arrr. I have dreamed of this day!'

212

'I too have dreamed of this day,' cried Miss Bronteen. 'I have dreamed of this day almost daily.'

'Arrr. So you'll sail with me to the ends of the earth?'

'In a heartbeat!'

More kissing ensued. Blades of grass were studied by one and all.

'I just have to nip back and fetch my books and then I'm ready to go,' said Miss Bronteen. 'Won't be a tick.'

'Books?' cried Crow's-Nest Jake to much muttering from the crew. 'Books? We'll have no books on board our ship.'

'No books?' said Miss Bronteen. 'Whatever can you mean?'

'Books is bad luck,' said the pirate. 'Everyone knows that.'

'No, they don't,' said Miss Bronteen. 'I don't.'

'Arrr, it's as true as I'm standing here,' said the Pirate Headmaster. 'Ain't that right, me hearties?'

'Arrr!' cried the crew.

'But I love books,' said Miss Bronteen.

'But you have me now,' said the pirate, holding out his hand. 'Ain't that enough?'

Miss Bronteen looked at him for a very long time.

'Frankly, no,' she said, before turning on her heels and walking away.

Sponge became over-emotional and accidentally fired both his pistols, putting a hole through one of Captain Cutlass's tail feathers and knocking himself and Mildew into the nearby shrubbery. When Mildew emerged, groaning and staggering about, he had a mouthful of greenery, giving the startling impression of a large and bushy beard.

'Arrr!' cried the Pirate Captain in terror. 'It's Greenbeard come back from his watery grave!'

The pirates stared wide-eyed, then turned and ran in a wild panic, disappearing down the drive like a whirlwind. Mildew spat the foliage out of his mouth and grinned. Sponge patted him on the back.

'Well done, Mildew,' he said.

'Thanks, old sandwich.'

Trained Monkeys

The Chair of Governors marched towards the Headmaster, who instinctively raised his cutlass ready for another battle. The teachers rallied to his side. The governors lined up against them. Sir Brashly smiled and held up his hands.

'At ease, soldiers,' he said.

With some reluctance the staff lowered their weapons, still eying the governors with suspicion.

'I am impressed, sir,' said Sir Brashly. 'Very impressed.'

'You are, sir?' said the Headmaster proudly. 'I had thought you believed this school to be soft.'

'Well, I was wrong, man!' said Sir Brashly. 'Why, if I'd had a few more in my battalion like these men of yours, the Empire would be twice the size! That French chap is terrifying.'

'That's Miss Bleu, our French teacher.'

'Good Lord,' said Sir Brashly. 'I've rarely seen the like, Headmaster. I think I may have underestimated you and your school.'

'Thank you, sir,' said the Headmaster.

'And dashed smart thinking to have trained monkeys about the place. I tried the same thing at the Siege of Mohair but the little blighters ran off.'

'Trained monkeys, sir?' said the Headmaster.

The Chair of Governors pointed to Mildew and Sponge and the rest of the boys.

'There, man,' he said. 'Are you blind?'

'They are students at the school, sir,' said the Headmaster.

'You're wasting your time,' said Sir Brashly. 'I tried to teach a monkey basic geometry once. They simply won't sit still.'

'We also have that problem, sir,' said the Headmaster.

'Well, I think I speak for the rest of the governors when I say that a school capable of fending off an attack by pirates can't be doing much wrong and I shan't be the one to close it down, sir.'

Tears glistened in the Headmaster's eyes.

'There is still the matter of the money for the

building work, Sir Brashly. I regret to inform you that –'

'Yes, yes,' said Sir Brashly, waving the Headmaster's words away. 'Of course, of course. We'll find you the money you need. I'm fabulously wealthy and alarmingly impetuous. The money will be with you tomorrow!

'Now, then, we really ought to let you get on. I think we've seen all we needed to.'

Mildew and Sponge started to walk away when the Headmaster relieved them of their weapons and pirate garb.

'For the best, I think,' he said.

Mildew and Sponge nodded. They had realised they weren't the weapon-carrying sort. Weapons, it turned out, were both frightfully dangerous and surprisingly heavy.

Kenningworth sidled over to them.

'Look,' he said quietly. 'I really haven't been following you, I promise.'

'But we saw you,' said Sponge. 'With our own eyes.'

'I can't explain that,' said Kenningworth. 'But it's true, I swear. Whoever it was trying to foil your attempt to find the treasure, it wasn't me. I just wanted to clear that up before I left for the south of France.'

Mrs Kenningworth overheard and came to

speak to her son. 'Oh dear. I know you had your heart set on Le Petit Prince boarding school, but I don't think the Mediterranean climate would suit you – and besides, Sir Brashly Bugle has persuaded me that I should send you somewhere more challenging.'

'Where?'

'The Musket-Ball Military Academy in Basingstoke.'

'Basingstoke?' said Kenningworth tearfully. 'Basingstoke? I can't go to Basingstoke! I shan't go to Basingstoke! Never!'

'Hush, now,' said Mrs Kenningworth, looking round. 'You're causing a scene. I don't see what the problem is. You'll have a lovely time.'

'Mrs Kenningworth, I presume,' said Sponge.

'Why, yes,' said Mrs Kenningworth. 'Have we met?'

'We are friends of your son,' said Mildew.

Kenningworth stared at them in confusion.

'Well, aren't you going to introduce me to your friends, Ambrose?'

'Friends?' said Kenningworth, looking about him.

'Arthur Mildew,' said Mildew, holding out a hand. 'Of the Berkshire Mildews. Delighted to meet you, ma'am.'

'Algernon Spongely-Partwork,' said Sponge.

'What charming young men,' said Mrs Kenningworth. 'How lucky you are to go to a school with such admirable role models. It wouldn't hurt you to be a little more like them, Amby-Wamby.'

'But Mumsy –'

'Hush now,' said Mrs Kenningworth. 'Mother's talking.'

'We just wanted to say how sorry we'd be if Ambrose was to leave the school,' said Mildew, surreptitiously pulling out one of his nose hairs and weeping pitifully. Furthermore, Hipflask, Enderpenny and Filbert came over to see what the fuss was about.

Mrs Kenningworth's eyes brimmed with tears.

'Oh, my,' she said. 'Ambrose. Look at the effect your mooted departure is having on these poor darlings. Why did you pretend you were lonely when you are so loved?'

'I, er, don't know, Mother,' said Kenningworth.

'Well, I simply won't rip you away from the arms of your chums,' she said. 'I simply won't. It's too cruel. You must stay and I won't hear another word about it!'

Mrs Kenningworth rejoined the other governors and Kenningworth, Mildew and Sponge watched her go.

'Your mother seems very nice,' said Mildew. 'For a parent.'

'I can't believe I'm going to have to stay in this dreary hellhole with you weevils,' said Kenningworth.

'Charming young men, I think you meant, Amby-Wamby,' said Sponge.

Kenningworth rolled his eyes and wandered off. But they saw a smile play across his face as he did so.

'I'm not sure Kenningworth was as keen to go elsewhere as he pretends,' said Mildew.

'I know,' said Sponge. 'Or at least not to a place where they make you march up and down at six o'clock in the morning.'

The governors roared away in their carriage, spraying gravel and dust in their wake.

24
Kenningworth Unmasked

The boys were given the rest of the day off while the teachers took back possession of the school, and though Mildew and Sponge searched for him everywhere, not a trace could be found of Newboy.

'Well, I suppose that's the end of another adventure,' said Mildew.

'Perhaps,' said Sponge. 'Although it's a bit odd, isn't it?'

'What is?' said Mildew.

'That Greenbeard's treasure should have been in exactly the same place that Flintlock first buried Mr Particle.'

'Yes,' said Mildew, stroking his chin. 'I suppose that is odd, now you mention it.'

'I mean, there must be a mistake somehow,'

said Sponge. 'Or the treasure has long since been stolen.'

'Wait!' said Mildew. 'They did find something. They found the bust of you, Sponge!'

'Of course!'

The boys went to the entrance hall, where the Roman bust of Sponge stood on its plinth. Sponge smiled as he always did, recollecting his trip to Roman times and his moment of heroism. Mildew paced back and forth, peering at the bust.

'But it still makes no sense,' said Mildew. 'The treasure of the *Golden Skull* is supposed to be jewels. What has this bust got to do with anything?'

Mildew flailed in disappointment and one of his flailing hands hit the bust painfully.

And calamitously.

The bust teetered, and though it looked as if it was going to right itself, one last wobble sent it tumbling from the plinth and on to the grey flagstone floor, where it smashed into a thousand marble shards.

'My bust!' cried Sponge tearfully. 'Look at my bust!'

'Sponge!' shouted Mildew, pointing at the shattered fragments at their feet.

'I can't!' said Sponge. 'It's too horrible, Mildew.'

'No – look!'

Sponge opened his eyes and looked where Mildew's pointy finger was pointing. In among the shattered marble were dozens and dozens and dozens of sparkling gemstones, many of them very large indeed.

'It's the treasure!' shouted Mildew.

'So it is!' cried the Headmaster, looming over them with a greedy smile. 'Excellent. Miss Pernickety, get Mr Scurry to fetch a dustpan and brush – and something to put the precious stones in.'

'Greenbeard must have hollowed out my head and filled it with jewels,' said Sponge. 'Maybe it had been dug up years ago, Mildew. By Lord Mandrake or some such. Maybe it was already in the house.'

'One can only speculate at this point,' said the Headmaster. 'All that matters is that the jewels now belong to the school.'

Mr Scurry arrived and began sorting through the debris, collecting the jewels and placing them carefully in a velvet bag.

'I wonder,' said Mildew with a cough, 'if the treasure might not, in fact, be mine. Being a descendant of Greenbeard.'

The Headmaster smiled indulgently.

'Hmmm,' he said, tapping the tips of his fingers together. 'That is an interesting point, Master Mildew. Although I wonder if it would not actually be your father who would have the greater claim.'

'Well ...' said Mildew.

'And then there is, of course, the matter of these gems having been stolen from their rightful owners. Perhaps we ought to trace their descendants and see if they would be happy for you to inherit the jewels from the thief who stole them.'

'Is that what you're going to do?' said Sponge. 'Trace the real owners, sir?'

The Headmaster sniffed and adjusted his tie.

'No, Master Spongely-Partwork,' said the

Headmaster. 'I am going to sell them and repair the shoes – I mean, school.'

'But –' began Mildew.

'No more butting,' said the Headmaster. 'Off to bed now. You've had a very tiring day.'

'It's two thirty in the afternoon,' said Mildew.

The Headmaster did not reply but smiled his horrible smile until the nerve of both boys broke and they scampered away. They came to a halt in the cloisters.

'Ah well,' said Mildew with a sigh. 'It seems as though, against all the odds, everything has sorted itself out, Sponge, your busted bust notwithstanding.'

Sponge was forced, reluctantly, to agree. The school had once again been saved. Just then they heard the Headmaster shout for Mr Scurry. Then shout again.

Mr Scurry passed the two boys at speed carrying the velvet bag they had seen him with a moment before. 'Mr Scurry,' said Sponge. 'I think the Headmaster –'

Mr Scurry scurried on without responding.

'How rude!' said Sponge.

Mildew then noticed that another Mr Scurry was pushing a wheelbarrow across the quad.

'Sponge!' he cried. 'You know how there were two Kenningworths? There now seem to be two Mr Scurrys. And I think one of them is making off with the jewels!'

'Which one?' said Sponge.

'The one with the velvet bag full of jewels,' said Mildew. 'Come on!'

Sponge scampered after Mildew and as they turned the corner, they saw Mr Scurry duck into an empty classroom. They paused at the doorway before bursting in.

'Stop!' cried Mildew.

To their astonishment they found Mr Scurry inspecting the sparkling contents of the velvet bag.

'Thief!' shouted Mildew.

'Mr Scurry, how could you?' said Sponge.

Mr Scurry turned to them with hands on hips, an expression of haughty disdain on his face.

'Ha!' said the caretaker. 'Fools! I am not, in fact, Mr Scurry at all!'

With that, he pulled off a mask and threw it to the floor.

'Kenningworth!' cried Mildew and Sponge.

'The very same!' cried Kenningworth.

'You monster!' shouted Sponge. 'We just helped you avoid being locked away in a military academy!'

'You'll never get away with it, Kenningworth!' cried Mildew.

'Never get away with what?' came a voice from behind them.

Mildew and Sponge turned to see another Kenningworth walking towards them through the door.

'What? How? Which? What?' burbled Sponge.

'Two Kenningworths?' said Mildew. 'What madness is this?'

'That's not me!' shouted the most recent Kenningworth. 'I'm me!'

'That's easy for you to say,' said Mildew.

'I'm telling you,' said this Kenningworth, 'that is an imposter. Look at his hair. It's ridiculous!'

They all turned to face the other Kenningworth, who had now put all the jewels in the bag.

'Ha!' he cried. 'Fools! I'm not Kenningworth at all!'

Kenningworth's imposter pulled off a mask and threw it away.

'Newboy!' cried Sponge and Kenningworth.

'So it was you following us!' said Mildew.

'Yes!' said Newboy. 'I let you lead me right to the treasure.'

'I knew you were up to no good!' cried Mildew.

'No, you didn't,' said Sponge. 'I did.'

'I strongly suspected it.'

'I'm not at all sure you did,' said Sponge. 'You never mentioned it.'

'I had an inkling, Sponge,' said Mildew. 'A rather intense inkling.'

'Er ... Newboy is getting away,' said Kenningworth.

'Let's get after him, Sponge!' said Mildew. 'Kenningworth, go and tell the Headmaster that you – I mean Newboy – is escaping with the jewels.'

'Why should I do anything ...? Oh, all right.'

Kenningworth ran off to the Headmaster while Sponge and Mildew headed after Newboy.

Balloon

Mildew and Sponge ran outside but there was no sign of Newboy anywhere.

'Where on earth can he have got to?' said Sponge.

'He's as slippery as an eel, Sponge,' said Mildew. 'But we'll track him down. Or my name's not Arthur Mildew!'

'To think that Newboy was tricking us all along,' said Sponge.

'Indeed,' said Mildew. 'And to think you wanted to make him your second-best friend.'

'So did you,' said Sponge.

'Well …' said Mildew. 'I don't think I shared your enthusiasm.'

'But–' said Sponge.

'I don't think us arguing is going to find

Newboy, is it, Sponge?' said Mildew. 'Let's put it all behind us.'

Sponge scowled at Mildew but saw something move over his friend's shoulder.

'There!' he cried.

Sure enough, Newboy had been hiding behind a box hedge and Mildew strode across to confront him.

'Give up, Newboy!' cried Sponge.

'Ha!' said Newboy. 'Fools! My name is not Newboy at all!'

As he said this, he tugged at a place behind his ear and pulled off what turned out to be yet another mask.

Long auburn tresses fell about the shoulders of he – or she, as it now became clear – whom they had once known as Newboy.

'I am none other than Felicity Fallowfield, arch criminal and master of disguise!'

'Shouldn't that be mistress?' said Sponge.

'No,' said Felicity Fallowfield. 'I am using master in the sense that I have mastered it – not in the sense that I am a female counterpart to the master of a house. It doesn't carry the same weight at all.'

'I can see that,' said Sponge.

She tossed her head. The two boys gasped as the light played across Felicity's silken hair. She rolled her eyes and, with a series of flick flacks, disappeared from view.

The two boys stood dumbfounded.

'Felicity Fallowfield,' said Mildew dizzily.

'Yes,' said Sponge. 'Why are you looking like that? That's what Mr Luckless used to look like when he was going all gooey over Miss Livia.'

'Nonsense,' said Mildew, shaking his head. 'I don't know what you're talking about. We must discover her hairabouts – whereabouts – and apprehend her, Sponge. Quickly!'

The boys rushed off in the direction Felicity Fallowfield had taken, running into the kitchen garden with its high brick walls, but once again she seemed to have disappeared.

'Can you hear something?' said Sponge.

Even as Sponge said this, a shadow passed over them, and when they looked up to see what might be causing it, they saw Felicity Fallowfield drifting by in a hot-air balloon.

'So long, boys!' she cried, grinning. 'Maybe we'll meet again one day!'

Mildew stared up.

'You'll never get away with it!' he shouted.

'What?' shouted Felicity Fallowfield, her voice now very faint.

'I said, you'll never ... Oh, never mind,' shouted Mildew. 'She's got away with it completely.'

'What are we going to do now, Mildew?' said Sponge.

'I don't know, Sponge,' he replied. 'I don't know. It looks as though Felicity Fallowfield has done it again.'

'Stop admiring her, Mildew. She's taken the treasure,' said Sponge. 'We've failed. We've had the means to save the school in our hands twice – and lost it both times.'

'To be fair, the parcel of money from the time machine was never actually in my hands, Sponge. And the jewels were in your bust, so …'

Sponge tried to adopt an expression to indicate that he wasn't going to grant these comments the dignity of a response, but Mildew was already wandering off.

'We'd better inform the Headmaster that far from Newboy being the thief, it was in fact Felicity Fallowfield.'

'Yes,' said Sponge. 'Newboy was innocent all along. I'm glad. I liked him.'

'You do realise there never was a Newboy?' said Mildew. 'He was entirely fictitious. It was Felicity Fallowfield all along. She must have read about the treasure in the *Daily Wail*, just like the pirates.'

Sponge stopped for a moment, deep in thought.

'Of course,' he said. 'I knew that. Shame. I rather liked him.'

Mildew rolled his eyes.

'Who could have guessed that Felicity Fallowfield would escape in a balloon,' said Sponge.

'Sponge?' said Mildew, as though he had only just that moment recognised his friend. 'Where's Newboy?'

Sponge stared at him.

'What on earth do you mean, Mildew?' he replied. 'You just told me there was no Newboy.'

'No Newboy?' said Mildew. 'Whatever can you mean? Of course there's a Newboy. Small chap, about yay high.'

'Has Felicity Fallowfield driven you loopy?' said Sponge.

'Felicity Fallowfield?' said Mildew. 'What? What has Felicity Fallowfield to do with anything? I don't know what you're talking about.'

'How could you not know?' said Sponge in amazement. 'We've just watched Felicity Fallowfield escape.'

'Felicity Fallowfield?' said Mildew. 'Escape? Are you quite well, Sponge?'

'Am I quite well?'

'Really?' said Mildew. 'You seem confused.'

'I seem confused?'

'Yes – you keep repeating everything.'

'Repeating everything?'

'Yes.'

'Never mind that!' cried Sponge. 'Newboy wasn't Newboy at all. In fact he wasn't any kind of boy, but a girl. And a girl called Felicity Fallowfield. She claims to be a master criminal. How could you forget all that?'

Mildew frowned.

'I don't think I would forget. Are you sure I was here?'

'Of course you were here,' said Sponge. 'It only just happened. She has just this minute left by balloon.'

'Ah, Sponge,' said Mildew. 'Where's Newboy?'

Sponge stared at him.

'I think you may have taken leave of your senses, Mildew.'

'What on earth can you mean?' said Mildew.

'You have just seen Newboy revealed as a master criminal and, more disturbingly still, as a girl.'

'A girl?' cried Mildew. 'I think it's you who have taken leave of your senses.'

'But you saw it with your own eyes, Mildew,' said Sponge. 'Saw her escape in the balloon.'

'Sponge!' cried Mildew. 'Good to see you. Any trace of Newboy at all?'

Sponge stared at him for a long time. Mr Luckless

walked by, looking at his pocket watch.

'Everything all right, boys?' he said, walking on without waiting for a response.

'Of course!' cried Sponge. 'This is about you being hypnotised. There's always a key word that hypnotists use when they wake their victim. It makes you forget everything that's just happened.

'Felicity Fallowfield posing as Newboy posing as Kenningworth must have used that word – the "b" word. The one that makes you keep forgetting where you are.'

'Blood?' said Mildew, catching his friend as he swooned.

'No,' said Sponge woozily. 'The other "b" word – the word for round, floaty things …'

'Bubbles?'

'Oh, for goodness' sake,' said Sponge. 'You inflate them. Or sometimes they are inflated by hot air and have a basket underneath for people to travel in.'

'Oh,' said Mildew. 'A ba–'

Sponge slapped his hand over his friend's mouth to stop him saying the word.

'Otherwise we'll have to go through it all again,' said Sponge.

'Understood,' said Mildew. 'And that word made me forget?'

'Yes,' said Sponge. 'It's all in the book.'

'I'm not sure I entirely understand,' said Mildew.

Sponge reached forward and ruffled Mildew's hair into a furry ball and tweaked his nose.

'Now see here,' said Mildew, trying to locate Sponge through the mass of hair covering his eyes.

Sponge stamped on his toe making Mildew cry out.

'Sponge?' he cried. 'What are you doing?'

'Balloon,' replied Sponge.

'Ah. Any sign of Newboy?' said Mildew.

Sponge smiled and calmly explained everything to Mildew, while taking special care not to mention the word 'balloon'.

'Extraordinary,' said Mildew. 'Any idea why my toe hurts?'

'No,' said Sponge quietly.

Mildew peered at him.

The boys went to the Headmaster's office to find him returned to his usual good humour. Kenningworth was there too.

'I'm afraid we lost the treasure, sir,' said Mildew.

'Yes,' said the Headmaster. 'Kenningworth tells me Newboy the new boy was a master criminal.'

'In a manner of speaking, sir,' said Mildew. 'Newboy was actually Felicity Fallowfield.'

'Felicity Fallowfield?' said the Headmaster. 'My goodness. I've read about her exploits. Did you manage to stop her at all?'

'I'm afraid not, sir,' said Sponge. 'She gave us the slip in a ba– … She gave us the slip, sir.'

'Yes,' said Mildew. 'She escaped with the treasure. The lot, sir. I'm afraid all our efforts were in vain.'

'Ah, well,' said the Headmaster. 'Sir Brashly Bugle has kindly agreed to forward the necessary funds for repairs, so we can still live to fight another day. I think we owe Kenningworth here an apology. Felicity Fallowfield, a.k.a. Newboy, was using him as a cover for her deceitful doings.'

'Yes – sorry, Kenningworth,' said Mildew.

'Apology accepted,' said Kenningworth with a thin smile.

'Although,' said Sponge, 'Kenningworth was the one who sold the story to the *Daily Wail* and alerted both the pirates and Felicity Fallowfield to the presence of the treasure at Maudlin Towers.'

'Yes,' said Mildew. 'That was the real Kenningworth – this Kenningworth.'

'Without him none of this would have happened,' said Sponge. 'We might have found the treasure unhindered and saved the school.'

'Hmmm,' said the Headmaster. 'You have a point.'

'Apology retracted,' said Mildew.

Kenningworth shrugged and walked away with a smile. Mildew and Sponge broke into a smile themselves. Everything did indeed seem to be back to normal.

'Incidentally, sir,' said Mildew. 'Why was there a burn mark on the rug in the hall if the combusting was a ruse?'

'I'm afraid that was Mr Lithely,' said the Headmaster. 'He really did spontaneously combust. I think it's all that energy he had. Just went up in flames as soon as the pirates attacked. I suppose I shall have to find yet another sports teacher for Maudlin Towers.'

Mildew and Sponge nodded and hoped this would not be a special priority of any kind.

Biscuits

The following morning, Mildew and Sponge sat with the other boys discussing the events of the previous days.

'Arrr. Fancy Newboy fooling us all like that,' said Enderpenny.

'Pah!' said Kenningworth. 'I never trusted him. There was something about the eyes.'

'You didn't say anything, matey,' said Furthermore.

'I was biding my time,' said Kenningworth.

'Ha!' said Mildew.

'Don't ha me, Mildew,' said Kenningworth. 'Felicity Fallowfield led you a merry dance. If I hadn't come in, you'd still think she was me.'

'Well, at least the pirates be gone,' said Filbert. 'I think Mildew and Sponge be needing a bit of credit for that.'

'Arrr. I quite liked the pirates,' said Footstool.

'Aye. So did I, shipmate,' said Furthermore.

'Arrr, and they were going to extend and enrich the curriculum,' said Hipflask, 'to accommodate the less academically-minded students. There was going to be a module on sea shanties.'

'And Mr Jake's tales of terror were horribly good,' said Enderpenny. 'That one about flesh-eating sea snails ...'

There was a collective shudder.

'They were, however, talking about throwing us all off the Trembling Tower,' said Mildew. 'So ...'

'And blowing up the school,' Sponge added.

'Maybe at the same time,' said Mildew.

The boys were forced to agree that there were downsides to a pirate regime. The conversation went on until Mildew and Sponge wandered off and sat on their own at the edge of the sports field, looking out towards the bothy.

'So, Sponge,' said Mildew. 'We have saved the school again.'

'Yes,' agreed his friend. 'I think we did. After a fashion.'

'We saved it from pirates, a werewolf (again) and, perhaps most heroically of all, from school governors.'

Sponge shuddered at the mention of governors.

'But not from Felicity Fallowfield,' he said.

Mildew blushed. Then he blushed a second time at the thought of blushing the first time. Sponge also blushed – as he always did when he saw someone blush.

'Felicity Fallowfield has beaten the best detectives in the world, Sponge,' said Mildew. 'No shame in that.'

Sponge nodded.

'And what of that giant floating eyeball, Mildew?'

'It's waiting for us, Sponge,' said Mildew. 'But we shall be ready for it.'

'Shall we?' said Sponge doubtfully.

'We have the advantage, Sponge,' said Mildew.

'We do?'

'We know it's coming,' said Mildew.

'Although not exactly when,' said Sponge.

'True,' said Mildew.

'Or why,' said Sponge.

'There is that, yes,' agreed Mildew.

They thought about this for a moment or two before deciding that this was one of those things that seem better if you didn't think about it very much.

A little while later, back in the dormitory, Sponge walked over to Mildew's bedside locker and with Mildew gazing on in astonishment, proceeded to take a packet of biscuits from the drawer. Sponge

 selected one and began to nibble.

'Sponge,' said Mildew. 'I don't wish to alarm you, but you appear to be eating my biscuits.'

Sponge wiped the crumbs from the corner of his mouth and sighed happily.

'Sponge!' said Mildew.

'Balloon,' said Sponge.

'Hello, Sponge,' said Mildew. 'What's happening?'

'It seems you're sharing your biscuits with me.'

'Am I?' said Mildew. 'That's very generous of me.'

'Yes,' said Sponge.

'But then I am a very generous person, Sponge.'

'Yes,' said Sponge. 'Yes, you are …'

The two friends ate their biscuits in contented silence, each of them wondering what strange and mysterious occurrences would be waiting for them in their next adventure …

Maudlin Towers
Near Lower Maudlin
Cumberland
England

Ahoy there Parents! ✸

Arrr! There be much excitement here
at Maudlin Towers. As usual we be not
allowed to go into details but I will just
say that ~~————————~~ and ~~————————~~
Hard to believe, I know!

Sponge and I have saved the school.
Again! Not so much as a biscuit in
reward. Arrr!

Fondest regards
Arthur Mildew Esq
x x x

PS Please send more biscuits
PPS Arrr!

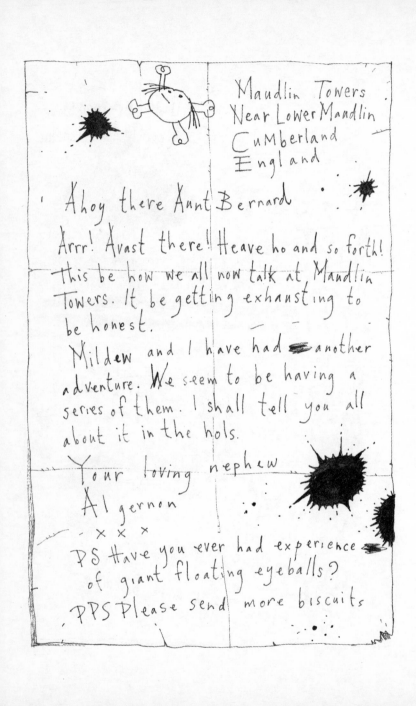

Maudlin Towers
Near Lower Mandlin
CuMberland
England

Ahoy there Aunt Bernard

Arrr! Avast there! Heave ho and so forth!
This be how we all now talk at Maudlin
Towers. It be getting exhausting to
be honest.

Mildew and I have had another
adventure. We seem to be having a
series of them. I shall tell you all
about it in the hols.

Your loving nephew
Algernon
x x x

PS Have you ever had experience
of giant floating eyeballs?

PPS Please send more biscuits

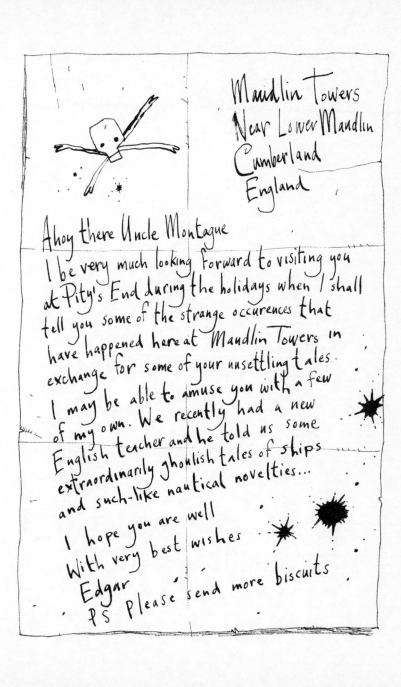

Maudlin Towers
Near Lower Maudlin
Cumberland
England

Ahoy there Uncle Montague

I be very much looking forward to visiting you at Pity's End during the holidays when I shall tell you some of the strange occurences that have happened here at Maudlin Towers in exchange for some of your unsettling tales. I may be able to amuse you with a few of my own. We recently had a new English teacher and he told us some extraordinarily ghoulish tales of ships and such-like nautical novelties...

I hope you are well
With very best wishes
Edgar
PS Please send more biscuits

MAUDLIN TOWERS

is riddled with mysteries ...

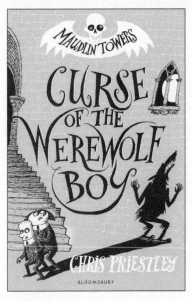

Is that a Viking in the school grounds?

Could there be a ghost in the attic?

Is there a werewolf wandering the corridors?

Why has the history teacher stopped being boring?

More importantly, who has stolen the School Spoon?

Can Mildew and Sponge save the day (and Christmas)?

A time-travelling, brain-boggling, mirth-making
adventure awaits!

Mildew and Sponge will return in another *Maudlin Towers* adventure riddled with mystery …

COMING SOON

THE AUTHOR

About the Author

Chris Priestley was born and grew old. He has lived in various places for varying amounts of time. He enjoys eating toast and looking at things. Despite all attempts to stop him, he has written and illustrated this book himself. The relevant authorities have been alerted.

Do you dare read all the
Tales of Terror?

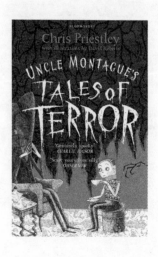

Edgar can't resist the strange and twisted stories his Uncle Montague tells when he goes to visit him in his creaky old house. Tales of gruesome curses and unquiet ghosts trip off his tongue. He seems to have an endless supply.

But what is Montague's own connection to the spine-chilling stories he spins? As night draws in, Edgar begins to suspect that his uncle has saved the most terrifying twist till last …

'Genuinely spooky' Charlie Higson

'Scare yourselves silly' *Observer*